# The Y-Plague

Marzie G. Crown



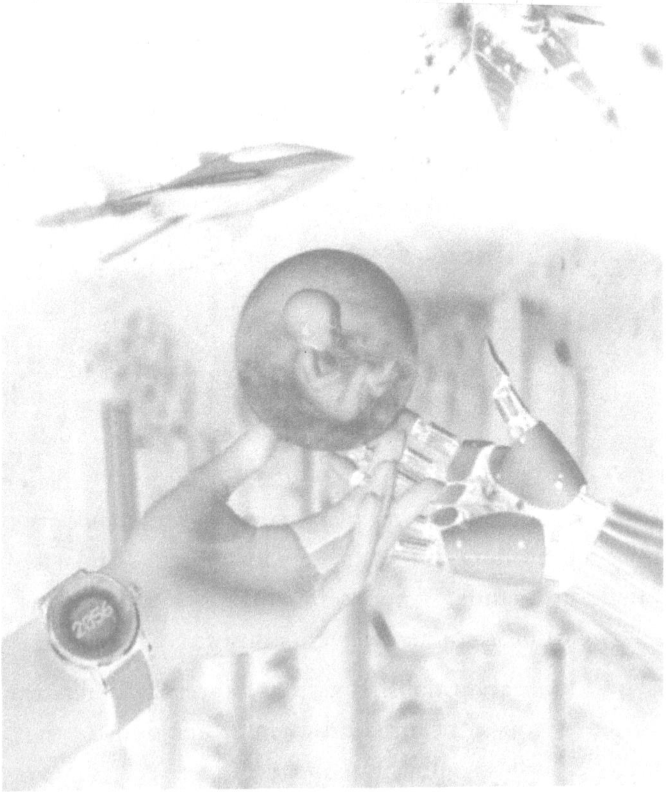

**ISBN: 979-8-9946849-0-0**

**First Edition**

---

**Disclaimer**

# Dedication

For those who bore the future
when survival demanded the unthinkable.
For the mothers of a world that could not wait.
And for the children who will never know
what it cost to keep them alive.

# Epigraph

*"Extinction is rarely sudden.*
*It arrives in choices—*
*each one reasonable,*
*each one irreversible."*

— Marzie G. Crown

# Acknowledgment

I extend my deepest gratitude to Yvonne Jayne, Carola Binski, Missi Wheeler and Jeff Purser for their invaluable support and unwavering dedication. Their keen insights and guidance were instrumental in bringing The Y-Plague to life, and I am profoundly grateful for their commitment to this journey.

# Table of Contents

# Author's Note

This novel is a work of speculative science fiction rooted in extrapolated biology, epidemiology, artificial intelligence, and systems theory. While the science presented here is fictional, it is built upon real-world principles pushed to their ethical and physiological limits.

The story does not ask whether humanity can survive catastrophe, but whether survival itself can become a form of violence when it demands transformation, sacrifice, and loss on an unprecedented scale. The technologies depicted are not intended as predictions, but as thought experiments—tools to examine how desperation reshapes morality, identity, and consent.

Motherhood, in this world, is not an instinct but a responsibility imposed by extinction. Bodies become battlegrounds. Love becomes labor. And continuation carries consequences that echo far beyond birth.

This book is not an argument for any scientific path forward. It is a meditation on what happens when the future must be carried by those who never volunteered to hold it.

Any resemblance to real persons or institutions is coincidental. The emotional costs explored here, however, are very real.

# Prologue

The last natural-born men did not die quietly. They raged against extinction with protest, prayer, denial, and war. Governments collapsed beneath the weight of panic. Faith splintered. Science fractured into rival factions—some chasing salvation, others clinging to dignity in the face of inevitability. The end did not arrive as a whisper, but as screaming headlines, empty nurseries, and the slow, unbearable realization that no law, weapon, or border could halt biology's verdict.

When the final generation faded, the world did not end.

It endured.

For nearly two decades, humanity adapted to a future without fathers. Women governed, built, preserved, and remembered. Artificial intelligence filled gaps once occupied by instinct and inheritance. Children were raised by communities, by machines, by hope—but never by men.

Then came the serum.

The first child born from it was called a miracle. A singular success born from desperation and genius, known as the Serum Generation. Proof that extinction was not inevitable—only delayed. The world exhaled for the first time in years.

The second was labeled an anomaly.

The Phoenix Class rose from tragedy and sacrifice, their lives forged in loss before their first breath. They were fewer, fragile, and carried forward by grandmothers and machines. Still, they symbolized rebirth. Hope returned, tempered but alive.

It was only later—much later—that humanity began to understand the cost.

Because survival demanded more than innovation.

It demanded transformation.

And transformation always demands a price.

The future did not ask whether humanity was ready.

It simply arrived.

# Cast of Characters

The Inner Circle

**Dr. Anya Peters** — Protagonist; lead researcher.

**Captain Andrew Stone** — Astronaut; Anya's husband.

**Dr. Marsha Lee** — Anya's sister; scientist.

**Dr. Allen Lee** — Marsha's husband; scientist.

**Maya Lee** — Bioengineer; Anya's niece.

**Shelley Brown** — BioSkin developer; Maya's colleague.

Scientific Community

**Dr. Mona Cone** — Physician overseeing reproductive outcomes.

**Dr. Sharon Banker** — Chief Scientific Officer (New York).

**Florida Research Team** — Multidisciplinary scientists supporting Anya's work.

The Children

**Herma Stone (Andrew Herman Stone)** — Anya's child; first successful birth.

**Nova Stone** — Anya's grandson; Phoenix Class infant.

**Cindy Blaney** — Scientist; next generation researcher.

**Lynn Blaney** — Cindy's sibling.

Androids & AI Systems

**AI Central / Network Hub** — Global intelligence network.

**Caregiver Androids** — Including Cora, Lance, and Max.

**Medical & Service AIs** — Automated emergency and lab systems.

Extended Family & Others

**Barron Peters** — Anya's father.

**Felicia Brown** — Shelley's mother; BioSkin pioneer.

## Chapter 1

# Year 2056

"All the world's a stage, and all the men and women merely players" - *William Shakespeare.*

Anya, a striking woman in her mid-thirties with piercing blue eyes and raven-black hair that cascaded past her shoulders, hurried to her study after dinner. Activating her Ho3D, the 3D holographic communicator, she spoke in a dreamy-soft voice, "Hey, sweetheart. I'm missing you. Is it a good time to talk?"

The Ho3D unit hissed softly. Andrew Stone, a handsome man with a strong jawline, short sandy-blond hair, and broad shoulders, shimmered into existence, his image sharp but sensual, a perfect illusion of presence. "Hello, beautiful. Always," he replied.

Anya asked, "Are you ready to come home?"

Andrew smiled and said, "You have no idea. After a year, I can't wait to hold you and kiss you senseless."

Anya replied: "Me too, darling. I love you. How are Marsha and Allen doing?"

Andrew set down his mug. "I think they're chatting with Maya right now."

Anya picked up her hairbrush, stroked her hair, and asked, "Have you heard anything about your next gig after the Skypad 5 mission?"

Andrew lifted his drinking mug to his lips and replied, "Not a word yet."

"What about the anomalous sample we sent up? Any progress?"

Andrew crossed his fingers to show Anya: "Still working on it. Marsha feels hopeful. We have one more week before we're back, though."

Anya mirrored the gesture and said, "Me too. People down here are losing it." Her voice trembling, she asked, "Have you been watching the news?"

Andrew replied, "Yeah, it sounds rough, baby. What about your lab? Anything new?"

"Nothing concrete, darling. The sample we sent you is highly anomalous. I can't discuss the details right now, but I'm deeply worried."

"Well, if Marsha and Allen don't crack it, maybe the androids will."

"I saw three new containment zones flash on the city map today. It's becoming chaotic here, darling."

"One more week, sweetheart. Hang in there. I'll be home soon."

Anya cleared her throat, "Have you heard anything about your next mission?"

"Just that after we land, they'll do the health checks, then it's two weeks of vacation for yours truly." His eyes sparkled with playful intensity. "And trust me, I know exactly how I'm spending it."

Anya let out a soft laugh. "Yes … are we ready? With everything going on here?"

"We will find a cure, I know it. We've waited long enough, haven't we? It's time to start our family. I want a little girl with your eyes."

Anya projected a radiant smile across the holographic connection. "And I want a little boy as handsome as you, my darling. Do you know what tomorrow is, sweetheart?"

Andrew winked, "Yes, I remember, it's our fifth anniversary." He rotated his mug to show Anya the printed wedding image with a date on one side, and her birthday on the other. "I use the mug to remind me of the dates. I have a few surprises in store for you when I return. I'll talk to you in the morning. I hope to see you in that special little number."

Anya smiled. "You mean that red teddy?"

Andrew replied, "Oh, yeah!"

Anya laughed. "You read my mind."

An hour later, a wave of blown kisses ended the holographic call.

***

Anya returned to the living room where the newscast cast a dim glow on the television screen.

A young anchorman with a purple dyed comb-over reported, "In 2056, Earth faces an uncertain future. This highly contagious virus originated in overcrowded refugee camps in the Kurdistan Region. Initially dismissed as seasonal flu, symptoms like cough and fatigue spread rapidly due to cramped and unsanitary conditions, quickly devastating vulnerable children and older adults. The mortality rates have increased drastically in the past month. Airborne and a master of disguise, this virus hides within its victims, silently replicating and mutating. Transmission often occurs through direct contact or via air, spreading like an invisible wildfire into neighboring cities and towns. Border crossings, once paths of escape, have become hotspots for infection."

The anchorwoman, with intense dark eyes and a closely shaved head, added, "Despite advancements in AI protein prediction, a highly disturbing genetic anomaly now forces our attention closer to home. Dr. Anya Peters at the DNA Genome Laboratory in Florida discovered that the virus's genetic code resembles human DNA, suggesting it may invade human genetic material. Dr.

Peter's conclusive findings reveal that the virus exploits a critical vulnerability, rendering specific genes non-functional. Her report, the Y-Plague, predicts chilling, unavoidable implications: the eradication of the male gender."

Anya shivered and called out, "TV off."

The screen snapped to black, leaving the room silent. She retreated to bed, but the silence offered no refuge. All night, she tossed and turned, the word Y-Plague echoing in the darkness.

Chapter 2

# The Y-Plague

"The pestilence stalks in the darkness. In the most crowded places, our fear will have no refuge."
- Albert Camus, *The Plague.*

Long before sunrise, Anya left her restless bed, headed straight to her study, and commanded her unit: "Ho3D Activate."

The Ho3D projection shimmered across her wall, replacing the sterile darkness with scenes of humanity's panic. Anya watched the worldwide broadcast, observing the initial scramble as governments shut their borders and urged the public to wear masks. A flimsy shields against an unseen enemy. Data streams, news feeds, and the unfiltered terror of social media painted a starkly different picture: death counts spiraled, reflecting a chilling descent into the unknown. Global transit came to a halt, and the frantic pursuit of a vaccine, the only fragile thread of hope, fell short. The pathogen, a phantom menace, slipped through the cracks.

The public's outrage erupted in response to the leaders' dismissive statements, which now sounded like catastrophic miscalculations. Masks and vaccines created a mere illusion of safety, while the Y-Plague, a biological chameleon, mocked every defense. Horror turned into a grim spectator sport for the world as the horrifying truth became clear: the plague was a gendered apocalypse, relentlessly targeting and harvesting only those with the Y chromosome.

Anya watched the scenes unfold: hospitals had become charnel houses, and morgues were overflowing. Law and order had dissolved, replaced by a brutal struggle for survival. Men scattered like hunted animals, desperate to find refuge from the invisible reaper. Riots, looting, and the terrifying echoes of a collapsing society reached a shocking crescendo.

In the deep woods, some men built cabins for refuge, while others huddled in cold caves or abandoned buildings. Their whispered promises, "I'll be coming home soon," spun fragile threads against the impending silence. The primal urge to leave a legacy in the face of the encroaching void drove some men to desperate acts, such as impregnating a companion. Across the ravaged landscape, men became vagrants, their aimless wanderings a testament to a world collapsing around them.

Towns became silent graveyards, and prisons became dying tombs. Isolation became their final torment. The quiet sorrow of women, left to pick up the shattered pieces, replaced the laughter of men and boys day by day.

***

The morning light filtered through Anya's study window. It was nearly 6 a.m. The media's last image of a child weeping next to an empty chair burned into her memory. She called out to her Ho3D, "Turn off."

Chapter 3

# Skypad 5

"The best laid schemes o' Mice an' Men / Gang aft agley." - *Robert Burns, "To a Mouse."*

Four months after the discovery of the Y-Plague, despair gripped the globe. Anya, an expert in genomics and virology, led a team of forty-seven scientists in a tireless race to find a cure. At this point, only women remained in the lab, working two twelve-hour shifts daily, or even more. Every woman in Anya's lab had suffered a loss, whether it be family, friends, or acquaintances, and the weight of their grief hung heavily over them.

Captain Andrew Stone, Anya's husband, completed his mission in space. However, the crew chose to remain in orbit to avoid the contagion while searching for a cure, their lives abruptly confined to Skypad 5.

Anya's sister, Dr. Marsha Lee, a slender woman with bright, alert eyes, announced from Skypad 5 that they believed she had found a cure. A cheer erupted in Anya's lab, but within minutes, an alarm blared on Skypad 5, and Anya's emergency laboratory phone shrieked.

"Dr. Anya Peters," a woman's voice screamed on the line. "Multiple meteor showers have intersected trajectories. The kinetic impactors failed! Residual shrapnel projects a direct impact course with the Skypad 5 station!"

Anya dropped the receiver and turned to face her sister. Marsha's face looked confused on the screen. Anya screamed, "Send now!"

The Skypad 5 team rushed to upload the cure, but the monitor flashed, "Lost Connection." The lab grew quiet as Anya and her team scrambled to reestablish the connection. Only the soft, anguished whispers of her colleagues filled the air as they attempted to link to Skypad 5.

Anya shouted, "What happened? Did we get it?"

Dr. Dee, a scientist with long, neatly braided brown hair and dark-rimmed glasses, tapped at her console keys, trying to reestablish the connection. "I'm sorry, Dr. Peters, nothing has been received," she replied.

Anya scoured her team and ordered, "Try again!"

She watched as they scrambled to reconnect with Skypad 5. Grabbing the dangling phone receiver, she asked, "Can you reach them?"

"We're trying," replied the voice on the other end of the line.

Anya could hear a woman shouting orders to her crew: "Keep trying, and don't stop until I say so!"

Anya heard the voice on the line asking, "Would you like me to stay on the line with you?"

Anya replied, "Yes." She glanced at the screen that remained black. The frantic whispers stopped when her personal line rang. She answered it, whispering, "Maya?" All she could hear was sobbing. Anya said, "Please, answer me. Are you home? Are you okay?"

Maya managed a faint, "Yes."

"I'll call you as soon as I can," Anya promised before hanging up. At that moment, she heard someone call her name, "Doctor Peters, look!"

***

Anya quickly turned away from the black screen. Through the large plexiglass window, she saw a group of women in the media huddled outside, their attention focused on a particular spot. Anya's eyes widened. She moved to the lab door where Dr. Long, a tall woman with a commanding presence and close-cropped blonde hair, stood. The scientist swiped her passkey, and the lab door slid open. As the staff followed Anya, Dr. Dee remained at her console, repeatedly trying to reestablish a connection with Skypad 5.

Outside the lab, loud, terrifying voices echoed through the building's hallways. Anya and her team maneuvered between the media personnel and spotted a replay of the live stream on a small monitor. A catastrophic event was unfolding before them. Anya's face paled as she watched two meteors collide, shattering into fragments, ricocheting through space. A satellite near the space station captured the final images: shrapnel tore through Skypad 5, setting it to erupt into a fireball. The flames quickly extinguished moments before the impact silenced the recording satellite, and the broadcast went dark. Anya nearly collapsed, but her team members rushed to steady her.

Chapter 4

# How Many Today?

"Grief is the price we pay for love." - *Queen Elizabeth II.*

Anya barely heard her own voice. "I think everyone should go home, take a quick break, and return feeling refreshed," she suggested. A reporter interrupted, asking: "Did we get the vaccine?" Anya glanced back inside the lab, where Dr. Dee swiveled her chair to face Anya and shook her head, before returning to her console. The media crowded around them, shouting questions: "Dr. Peters, what are your plans now?"

"Will you continue the work?" another reporter asked. A third voice called out, "How do you feel about your husband's death?" Dr. Long, standing nearby, angrily shoved the reporter after hearing that question. From the back, near the televised screen, another reporter yelled, "Dr. Peters, wasn't that your sister, Dr. Marsha Lee, on Skypad 5?"

Anya, accompanied by her scientists, navigated through the media crowd without answering questions. The scientists moved back inside, and Dr. Long slammed the door behind them, shutting out the noise.

The media grabbed their equipment, scrambled down the hallway, and emptied the building.

"Anyone who wants to leave before the next shift can do so," Anya called out. "Dr. Croft's team will arrive here in 17 minutes. But before you leave, please ensure you upload all your data."

Anya asked Dr. Dee, "Anything?"

Dr. Dee rubbed at the bridge of her nose in a nervous gesture. Her lab coat was still unbuttoned as if she had never stopped moving. She met Anya's eyes and shook her head slightly. "I'm sorry. There's been no progress yet."

Dr. Long, taller and sharper in her movements, glanced at the wall clock before resting a steady hand on the back of Anya's chair. "I'll stay until the others arrive," she said gently. "You should go home, Anya. Maya needs you."

Dr. Blaney lingered near the terminal, fingers flying as she uploaded the last of the data. She was round-faced and warm, her reddish-brown hair pulled into a careful bun that never quite hid her exhaustion. "I'll head out after this finishes," she said with a soft smile. "The girls will be home soon, and um ..." She opened her arms and embraced Anya, who struggled to hold back her tears.

Dr. Gleeson, a young woman with a long blond braid and a tear-stained face, had not stopped crying since the spaceship explosion. She hugged Anya and blurted out, "I'm sorry for," but couldn't finish her sentence before she ran into the lab's bathroom, sobbing.

Mrs. Evans was Anya's lab secretary. A kind woman in her mid-sixties with a soft face and short, graying brown hair, opened the sealed door, her eyes visibly red from crying, and announced, "All the media have left. It is safe to go."

Mrs. Evans walked over to Anya and embraced her with a warm, sympathetic hug. With tears streaming down both of their cheeks, Mrs. Evans whispered, "I am so sorry, Anya."

Anya couldn't help but notice how much Mrs. Evans resembled her deceased mother. After their embrace, Mrs. Evans addressed the group, "The next shift is starting now. If anyone can cover Dr. Daily's shift for the next eight to twelve hours, please see me. I'm sad to report that her seven-year-old son, Kevin, has passed away."

A somber silence enveloped the room. Finally, Dr. Blaney said, "I'll take her shift."

Dr. Dee spoke up, "No, Liz, your husband passed away just last week. You need to go home and be with your girls. Plus, Dr. Daily's serum results are due in ..." Dr. Dee checked her watch…" in ten hours." I'm anxious to see them."

Dr. Granger, a nervous-looking woman in her late twenties with practical short light-brown hair, took Dr. Dee's place and immediately resumed her attempt to reconnect with Skypad 5.

***

The shock from the explosion, fused with an older, profound trauma, pulled Anya back into her past.

Mrs. Evans called out, "Anya!"

Anya watched Mrs. Evan's lips move through the fog of a clouded mind. A vivid memory of her mother surfaced, pulling Anya back to a time when they sat together discussing their plans for an upcoming weekend trip. Anya recalled how quickly her excitement had faded. At six, she came home from school to find her father standing between thirteen-year-old Greg and ten-year-old Marsha, who were crying the entire time. Her dad sat Anya down on the couch and informed her about her mother's fatal car accident, and that her soon-to-be-born baby brother wouldn't be coming home either. He held her tightly while she screamed.

Anya, overworked and overwhelmed, was on the verge of collapse. Her mind had tricked her into hearing her mother's voice, and she imagined her mother waving her hand over her face and calling out her name, "Anya." The sound faltered, reshaping itself into Mrs. Evans' voice calling her name.

"Anya?"

Anya instinctively responded, "Yes, Mom?" before realizing her mistake. The room went silent as Mrs. Evans and the team exchanged glances.

Mrs. Evans urged her, "Anya, you need to go home. Everything is under control. Your niece Maya needs you."

Upon hearing Maya's name, Anya focused, pressed a button on her watch to summon her car, and quickly removed her lab coat. Turning to Mrs. Evans, she asked the usual question, "How many today?"

"Mrs. Evans, with a somber expression, lowered her head and announced to everyone, "Twelve million died today, bringing the global total to 1.5 billion."

Chapter 5

# Carl-23

"The deeper that sorrow carves into your being, the more joy you can contain." - *Khalil Gibran.*

Anya emerged from the lab, her mind heavy with the day's grim tragedies. She approached her car, a sleek silver autonomous vehicle, which Anya had named Carl-23 after her twenty-third breakthrough achievement in her Cybernetic Automated Rapid Laboratory tests. This revolutionary device could detect the NZV virus within 3 minutes and had saved millions of lives 4 years ago.

The car's interior boasted plush seats and ambient lighting. When the door opened for her, she slid into the back seat. Carl-23 greeted her with a synthesized voice that sounded remarkably human-like.

"Welcome aboard, Anya," it said.

Anya's voice quivered with emotion. "Take me home."

A soft ping indicated that the passenger was seated in the perfect position, allowing Carl-23 to start the vehicle. As Anya traveled home, her mind raced with thoughts of Andrew and the months they had spent apart. Their last conversation took place the day before, when they had blown kisses to each other across the screen.

A vivid image flashed in her mind: Andrew dropped his mug on the floor. She watched the scene play out in slow motion, looping endlessly. The mug fell slowly, shattering the wedding image printed on it. Her sister, Marsha, looked confused while her brother-in-law, Allen, had a panicked expression after hearing the alarm.

In an instant, her thoughts went blank, much like the monitor she had seen in the lab. A wave of despair washed over her. Screaming, she curled into a fetal position in the backseat of the Carl-23 and cried.

Sensing Anya's distress, Carl-23 opened a compartment beneath the back seat, where a mechanism lifted a stack of tissues. Anya took a couple of tissues and said, "Thank you." Carl-23 recognized "thank you" as a task completed. It retracted its mechanism and closed the partition.

The car's anatomical gauge indicated Anya's distress, prompting it to adjust the cabin temperature to a more soothing level. A natural jasmine fragrance began to fill the interior.

Anya's favorite fragrances were jasmine, gardenia, and honeysuckle. The fragrance compartments were easily accessible for making changes. She remembered how Andrew occasionally, and mistakenly identified gardenia as honeysuckle, but the results were still favorable. Whenever Andrew caught a whiff of the honeysuckle on Anya, it signaled that she was in the mood for an evening of romance.

Carl-23 pulled up to Anya's house.

"Anya, you have arrived."

Anya, lying across the back, had gradually reduced her crying to a whimper. Her chest felt as if a sharp knife had cut deeply into her heart. Her mind raced. She heard her own thoughts, *'Are you done feeling sorry for yourself? You're not the only one who's lost someone.'*

Anya closed her eyes, took a deep breath, and released it, saying, "Stay in the moment. Stay focused, breathe."

She shook her loose hair away from her face. The sun reflected on her glossy black strands, creating the illusion of a blue satin sheet flapping softly in the wind.

She sat up, dried her face, and exited the Carl-23. The vehicle drove off to park in its designated spot.

***

Maya Lee, a beautiful, tall, and slender twenty-two-year-old specializing in robotic bioengineering, had long, wavy strawberry-blond hair and pale green eyes. Since joining the robotics program, she had become a bright light in Anya's life. As Maya peered out the window, Anya noticed her niece's face streaked with tears. Instantly, Maya burst out of the front door.

The two women embraced, their tears mingling. Anya held Maya tightly; their hearts felt heavy with the burden of their shared grief. They hurried inside the house, and Anya, worried that reporters might be lurking in the shadows, commanded, "Close the door!" The automated door shut behind them immediately.

Retreating to the living room, the weight of their sorrow was evident. The death toll was personal. Anya carried the heaviness of three losses: her husband, Andrew, her sister, Marsha, and her brother-in-law, Allen. Maya's grief ran even deeper, claiming four of the people she loved most: her parents, Marsha and Allen, her uncle Andrew, and her college boyfriend, Jeffrey, who had succumbed to the Y-Plague only days earlier.

The two women sat in silence, their minds racing with memories. They spoke of Andrew's infectious laughter, Marsha's unwavering strength, Allen's brilliant mind, and Jeffrey's witty comebacks.

"We'll get through this, Maya. Stay strong," Anya said.

Maya could only nod in response to her aunt's words. Anya whispered, "We must find the cure … we WILL find a cure!"

Chapter 6

# Max

"The best mirror is an old friend." - *George Herbert.*

The morning sun streamed through the holographic-shaded windows, activating at six a.m. and casting a soft, ethereal glow over the minimalist interior. Anya rubbed her tear-crusted eyes and noticed a figure standing by her bedside.

"Hello, Max."

"Good morning, Anya. Is there anything I can assist you with?"

"No, Max. We will go down to the kitchen."

Anya left the room, and Max, a utility android-model standing at 5'10" with a generic, non-humanoid face and rubbery skin lacking anatomical features, followed her down the stairs. Maya, who slept on the couch, stirred and opened her eyelids after a night of crying. The scent of fresh, warm pastries wafted through the air, pulling her from the depths of unrestful sleep. She got up and followed Anya and Max into the kitchen.

Anya whispered, "Morning," her voice laced with sadness. Maya nodded.

They heard a faint humming sound coming from a cylindrical kitchen device named Kit. Kit was preparing the programmed breakfast for Tuesdays: a steaming bowl of oatmeal, a side of fresh fruit, a pastry, and a cup of steeped herbal tea. The four-foot-tall metallic unit moved out of their way, shifting to the other side of the table.

The 3D holographic unit on the far kitchen counter displayed the current news. The grim headlines flashed as the anchorwoman with intense dark eyes and a closely shaved head announced, "The toll of the Y-Plague has surpassed two billion today. Twelve million more males died yesterday. After five months, hope for a cure remains elusive, especially now that the Skypad 5 station has exploded in space." The screen displayed a holographic image of the mission's group photo. Maya screamed, and Anya gasped, shouting, "Max, terminate the connection!" Max instantly obeyed.

Anya hugged Maya tightly before they left the kitchen. Kit noticed their absence and promptly recycled the uneaten breakfast, saving the essential components for later use.

As they entered the living room, they saw Liv, another metallic, cylindrical device, cleaning with precision. Liv's sensors detected their presence and adjusted the temperature to a comfortable level. Liv released a gentle lavender scent to create a relaxing atmosphere, then retreated to its solar recharging station in the hallway closet.

The women sat quietly in the living room until Maya's sobbing calmed down to a whimper. Anya's attention shifted to her android, "Max, please help me … Maya, I'm going upstairs. Are you coming too?"

Maya wiped her tears, nodded, replying softly, "Yes, I'll be up in a minute."

The android followed Anya to her bedroom.

"Max, I'm going to a funeral. Please retrieve a black dress and an appropriate accessory."

Max quickly went into Anya's closet, took out her clothes, and placed them on the bed. He chose matching jewelry from her vanity. Walking over to her, he gently put the earrings in her pierced ears. Stepping behind her, he placed a pearl-shaped hematite necklace around her neck; it was a gift from Andrew on their fourth anniversary. Afterward, Max returned with her polished shoes and purse.

"Thank you, Max," she whispered. "Check on Maya for me." Max responded in his soft, reassuring tone, "You're welcome. I will leave now."

He found Maya in her bedroom.

"I need your help, Max," she said, in a trembling voice. "Jeffrey's funeral is today. Please help me choose the appropriate outfit."

Maya pulled the towel off her head to dry her hair after her shower. Max returned from the closet and laid her clothes across the bed. Noticing Maya struggling with her tangled hair, he stepped forward and extended his hand. He took the comb and gently worked out the knots.

Maya's face was pale and drawn. She wore a simple black lace dress that fell to her knees, elegantly draping over her slender figure. Her long, flowing hair cascaded down her back, framing her delicate features. The contrast between the black fabric and her vibrant red hair revealed a striking beauty.

As Anya and Maya prepared to leave, Max approached them and asked in a soft, empathetic voice, "Is there anything else I can do for you?"

Anya replied, "Yes, Max, please summon our cars."

Max signaled for Carl-23 and Maya's car, Billy, to come from their parking area.

***

Cameras flashed as Anya and Maya stepped out of their front door. Microphones lined up close to their faces. The reporters blared into the mics, their voices clamoring with questions. Max loomed out of the shadows, his frame interposing itself between the women and the encroaching lenses.

Max spoke firmly but politely, "Please respect the privacy of these women." The reporters hesitated, startled by the android's imposing stature. Max's unwavering gaze silenced them. One reporter protested, "We're just trying to get a comment."

"Your questions can wait," Max replied.

Once the women drove away, Max returned inside, and the automated door closed behind him.

Chapter 7

# Lance

"The limits of the possible can only be defined by going beyond them into the impossible."
- *Arthur C. Clarke.*

At the Blaney funeral, a hollow weight settled in Anya's chest as she stood at the gravesite of Richard Blaney, the husband of her dear friend Liz. Liz, with tired eyes and a face weighed down by grief, had lost her partner to the devastating Y-Plague. This plague was draining the world psychologically, physically, and emotionally. Richard's funeral was a small affair, attended by only a handful of mourners.

As the mourners began to leave the gravesite, Dr. Blaney turned to Anya and said, "Thank you for coming, Anya. I didn't expect you to be here after …" She quickly changed the subject. She turned to her children and said, "Cindy, Lynn, look, Aunt Anya is here."

Cindy, a quiet seven-year-old with brown eyes and long, straight brown hair, remained silent. Her sister, Lynn, a four-year-old with bright hazel eyes and short, light brown curls, didn't say a word either.

Anya replied, "Liz, I'm sorry, but I can't stay."

"I understand."

Anya glanced at Liz's tear-streaked face, with her daughters clinging to her side. She inquired about Cindy, the older daughter. Dr. Blaney quietly confessed, "Cindy hasn't spoken a word since her father died."

***

*At Jeffrey's Funeral*—It was the ninth funeral Maya had attended in two weeks. Overwhelmed, she called Anya: "Aunt Anya, I'm heading back to the lab now. Can we talk later about holding a wake for my parents and Uncle Andrew?"

Anya replied, "Of course, Maya. I'm on my way to the lab too. See you soon."

***

Maya led the Robotics Research Department located next to Anya's research room. Her work was demanding and often stressful. She focused on enhancing

AI androids, including Lance, an impressive android with a well-defined, humanoid face, reddish hair styled in a men's undercut, and striking pale green eyes, representing a Max upgrade.

Maya's goal was to make these androids appear and behave more like humans. She envisioned AI playing a crucial role in developing a cure for the Y virus, which was a significant threat for the past five months.

At the DNA Genome Laboratory, Anya rushed into her lab building after yet another funeral. She dodged the relentless media and their unending questions, which blended into a chaotic surge of voices around her.

When the media appeared, Anya called out, her voice almost drowned by the noise, "Please, leave us alone. We're working on a cure. We will announce the news when we have it."

A terrible setback had thrown their research into chaos: an unknown contaminant once again compromised their latest experiment. Every lost hour dragged them closer to despair.

Anya announced to her team in a firm voice, "We can't let this setback derail our work. We must retest."

The team nodded, their faces showing determination. They were committed to working tirelessly, day and night, to overcome this obstacle.

In the adjacent room, Maya upgraded Lance's advanced program and made the final adjustments. Next, she started the new development testing, her voice filled with anticipation as she called out, "Lance."

The android responded in a smooth, masculine voice that sounded completely natural. "Yes, Maya, how can I help?"

Maya said, "Retrieve Billy and take me home."

Lance pressed his watch and directed Billy to meet them at the curbside. As Maya reached out and lightly touched Lance's arm, the android paused, processing his enhanced sensory capabilities, and waited for further instructions.

Maya tested Lance's newly developed sensitivity wiring when she asked, "How does it feel when I touch you?"

Lance turned his head to face her with a kind smile and replied, "I sense a gentle pressure against my exterior. It triggered my sensory response, indicating that I should pause and await your next request."

"Alright, Lance, come with me," Maya instructed.

Lance responded, "Okay."

Maya's car waited in front of the building. The android opened the back door so Maya could slide into the seat.

"No, Lance, I want to watch you drive Billy; I'll sit in the passenger seat," she said.

Lance closed the back door and opened the passenger door for Maya. As the android drove, Maya began writing in her notepad. After a moment, she tested his response by gently caressing his face.

While maintaining control of the vehicle, Lance asked her, "Yes, how can I help you?"

"How does it feel when my hand strokes against your face?" Maya asked.

Lance responded without turning his head: "I can feel your gentle touch on my right cheek."

"Maya pressed for more details. "Can you elaborate?"

Lance replied, "Your touch suggests that I should respond with a question."

Maya continued writing in her notepad, "Perfect." She placed her hand on the android's upper thigh. "How does this feel?"

Lance responded, "It indicates that I should ask you: was your touch an accidental movement?"

"No," she replied.

"Was your touch meant to signal me to pause and wait for further instructions?" he asked.

She noted their conversation and responded, "No."

"Are you touching me to provoke a sexual response?" Lance inquired.

Maya looked up at him and said, "Yes."

Lance asked, "Now?"

Maya gently pulled her hand away from the android, set down her pen, and turned away to look out the window. She gazed at the familiar town her parents had driven through on their way to the Kennedy Space Center for their Skypad 5 mission. Turning her focus back to the android, she said, "No, I'm just checking your responses. Lance, return us to the lab."

Chapter 8

# Echoes in the Static

"The future belongs to those who believe in the beauty of their dreams." - *Eleanor Roosevelt.*

*At Anya's home*–Maya shared her idea with Anya about holding a virtual memorial gathering instead of a traditional service. They spent the first hour using their Ho3D, a 3D holographic conference gadget. Initially, they contacted family members. who needed to attend the wake service. During the second hour, they reached out to close friends who invited others to say their final goodbyes.

After an emotional gathering, Anya and Maya found it challenging to sleep. To pass the time, Maya decided to showcase Lance's enhanced programming abilities and granted Anya access to his command protocols.

Anya stepped closer to the attractive, red-headed android, Lance, whose face bore strategically placed freckles. She gazed intently into his left pupil. Her warm breath brushed against his cheek, triggering a response from Lance. "Anya, I can feel your breath. Do you need me?" he asked.

Maya, feeling a surge of energy for the night, exclaimed, "Perfect."

Anya responded, "Yes, Lance, please turn on the TV and raise the volume by twenty percent." She observed the internal components of Lance's eye. The fiber-optic, multicolored elements sparkled and glimmered as the TV switched on. The flickering lights triggered a memory: the first Christmas after her mother had passed away, Anya had sat alone on the dark living room floor, weeping, as she stared at the tree's decorative lights.

The recollection filled her eyes with tears. She stepped back from Lance. Maya, absorbed in her tablet, didn't notice the tears streaming down Anya's face.

Lance increased the volume to twenty percent while Maya recorded his response time on her pad, saying, "Excellent! I'm pleased." She paired Lance with all the household devices, including Max, Carl-23, and Billy.

After leaving Lance's side, Maya and Anya went over to the couch to watch the latest news. Maya pointed out the new anchorwoman, saying, "She's new." Anya nodded in agreement.

***

The newscaster, Marion Shane, a woman with large brown eyes and thin red lips, announced in a somber tone: "Today's death toll stands at nearly 20 million, bringing the total number of male casualties worldwide to almost 3 billion since the first case of the Y epidemic. The significant decline in the male population has brought us to levels not seen since the 1960s. Never in history has there been a more tragic time reminiscent of the 1918 Spanish flu pandemic, which caused nearly 100 million deaths globally."

The newscaster continued, depicting a grim outlook for the world's future: "Women, left to pick up the pieces of a shattered society, are facing unprecedented challenges never before seen in humankind. Despite these overwhelming odds, women are showing remarkable resilience. They are learning to adapt to this new reality with the assistance of AIs. The loss of men has created a massive labor shortage, nearly crippling industries and disrupting supply chains. Fortunately, the support of androids and the use of robots have helped us avoid such dire outcomes."

The newscaster introduced Dr. Helen Frey, an expert in comparative genomics, and inquired: "Doctor Frey, some members of our audience have asked why the Y-Plague has not affected male animals."

Dr. Frey, who wore large pink-framed glasses accentuating her attractive cheekbones, explained, "The devastating impact of the Y-Plague on humans is due to its precise targeting of the Y chromosome. This genetic marker, which is unique to males, makes them particularly vulnerable to the virus's destructive effects. However, the Y chromosome is a relatively recent evolutionary development, and not all species possess it."

Dr. Frey adjusted her glasses as they slipped down her powdered face and continued, "Many animal species evolved alternative systems for determining sex that do not depend on the Y chromosome. These systems offer protection against the virus. Additionally, physiological differences between humans and animals may have influenced their varying levels of susceptibility."

The newscaster concluded, "Thank you, Dr. Frey. Now we go to our weather reporter, Susan Black."

Anya tested Lance: "TV off." Lance immediately shut down the program.

Maya's head rested on Anya's shoulder. Not wanting to wake her, Anya whispered, "Lance, carry Maya to her bed."

Lance walked over to Maya and gently lifted her off the couch. He carried her upstairs, laid her softly on the bed, and covered her with a blanket. Without any further commands, Lance stood vigilantly by her bedside through the night.

Chapter 9

# The Hurricane

"The best way out is always through." - *Robert Frost.*

Anya's heart raced as she pondered the recent breakthrough in the fight against the Y-Plague. A potential cure was just twenty-four hours away.

Six months after the Y-Plague swept across the globe, nearly thirteen million males were dying each day, totaling almost 3 billion globally. Males still survived in the wombs of expectant mothers, clinging to the fragile thread of gestation. Hospitals and laboratories struggled to keep male infants alive; they typically passed away within hours or days. Incubators merely prolonged the infants' suffering. Everyone worked tirelessly, denying themselves rest. The laboratory was a hive of constant activity, driven by the urgent quest for a cure. With over two billion women left on Earth, humanity faced extinction.

As Anya entered her building and passed through the robot security, she saw Mrs. Evans rushing toward her, panic on her face. "We must leave now! We are near the eye of a Category 3 hurricane; it's accelerating and closing in fast!"

Sirens blared around them. Anya had turned off the news before the weather report, so she was unaware that a hurricane was threatening the city. Meteorologists hadn't predicted the sudden change or the shift in atmospheric conditions; the storm defied established models.

People in the area began to evacuate the east coast of Florida. Anya's team hurried to upload their current research data to a secure cloud server while also gathering their most essential notes. Anya offered a safe place to stay to anyone who needed it. Grateful for her generosity, Mrs. Evans and Dr. Dee accepted her offer. The rest of the team quickly scurried out of the building. Anya found Maya in the adjacent room. "We need to get home immediately, Maya, and pack our bags. A hurricane is coming. We should head out to your parents' house."

"Aunt Anya, since we're heading to my house, I don't need anything, but I will bring Shelley with me."

"Alright, I'll stop by the house and bring Max along," Anya replied. The two women agreed to meet at a specific location.

The wind howled fiercely along the coast of Florida as rain began to fall. Carl-23, operating on autopilot, accelerated to 120 mph (approximately 193 km/h). Max sat in the passenger seat while Anya watched from the back window. Maya's car, Billy, kept pace behind them.

Dark clouds gathered overhead, and strong winds shook their vehicles. In the distance, debris flew through the air as the wind uprooted trees and splintered power poles, with power lines sparking and whipping around like lightning. As the storm intensified behind them, Carl-23 and Billy swerved quickly to avoid objects flying from all directions.

Meanwhile, Mrs. Evans and Dr. Dee arrived at Maya's house before the others. They used the passkey Maya had provided to enter. Maya's long-time friend and bioengineer team member, Shelley Brown, joined them.

***

*Maya Lee's Orlando Home*—As the storm raged outside, the scientists immediately immersed themselves in their work, finding solace in their tasks amid the chaos. They watched live-streamed footage of the hurricane wreaking havoc. On television, the anchorwoman informed the public about hurricane history, discussing "The Great Labor Day Hurricane of 1935," which left a path of destruction. The death toll was unprecedented, and the economic losses reached astronomical figures.

For four anxious, sleepless days, the women worked long hours, taking quick naps. They waited anxiously 50 miles away for the storm to pass, so they could return to the lab and test new theories. The dynamic duo of engineers, Maya and Shelley, concentrated on refining Lance's advanced AI capabilities. Lance, dressed only in boxer briefs, received the instruction, "Lance, walk up and down the stairs." Maya's voice filled with purpose.

The android moved with fluid grace, each step precise and deliberate. Shelley, who was almost as tall as Maya and had naturally curly brown hair pulled into a high ponytail, noticed a minor imperfection and asked, "Maya, have you seen the slight glitch in Lance's right foot as he went up the stairs?"

"Yes," Maya replied.

"It's a minor issue that we can easily fix. Lance, please recalibrate your algorithm. Adjust the motion of your right foot to match that of your left, and begin ascending the stairs again."

Lance, a towering android, complied with the command. His synthetic form, crafted from advanced materials, resembled a fit young man but weighed only a fraction of a human. His superhuman strength enabled him to lift objects thirty times his weight and sprint a mile in just ten seconds.

As Lance reached the top, he turned to face Maya and announced, "Waiting for further instructions."

Maya nodded, her gaze fixed on the android's movements. "Descend the stairs, Lance," she commanded.

Lance's descent was smooth as he reached the bottom of the steps. He waited for his following command, his expression neutral, yet pleasing to behold.

Hungry, Maya suggested, "I think this will do for now. Let's take a break for dinner and test more later."

Shelley, who was scanning the electronic components scattered across the table, nodded in agreement. "Sounds good to me."

Anya and Dr. Dee immersed themselves in their research, carefully reviewing data and tests to develop formulations for future testing.

Instead, Maya suggested, "How about we go out to eat? Is anyone interested in taking an hour off?"

"An hour sounds perfect," Anya replied. "I just need to freshen up first."

Mrs. Evans agreed, saying, "That sounds like a great plan." With that, the women retreated to their separate rooms.

Chapter 10

# Saboteur

"There is no great genius without a
touch of madness." - *Seneca.*

Tears mingled with the cascading water as Anya stood beneath the spray, cherishing the bittersweet memory of Andrew's touch. A rattle from the bedroom window startled her. "Hello?" she called out, stepping onto the cold tiles. Wrapping a towel around herself, she left the bathroom. Wariness washed over her. The window near Marsha's vanity sat ajar, papers scattered across the floor. As Anya gathered her notes, a prickle of unease crept over her skin. A knock interrupted her thoughts.

Anya tightened her towel and said, "Come in."

Mrs. Evans stepped inside, a hopeful smile lighting up her face. "The hurricane has subsided," she announced. "They're assessing the damage; people can return in two days."

***

Anya asked the question that had been forming in her mind as she picked up the papers scattered on the floor. "Did you come in earlier?" She smoothed the papers and stacked them neatly on the vanity.

"No, why?"

"Did you see anyone up here?"

"No, Maya and Shelley are downstairs waiting. I heard Dr. Dee was singing in the shower when I knocked on her door to deliver the news."

The women had dinner at a quiet Chinese restaurant where the only sound was the clinking of utensils. They returned quickly to the house, their minds heavy with thoughts of the storm and the twenty-two reported deaths. Each of them retreated to their work.

Maya, reserved and thoughtful, found comfort in her friendship with Shelley, a vibrant 22-year-old colleague. Both came from scientific families and had maintained close friendships since third grade.

***

In Allen's study, Anya spoke into her Ho3D unit with Dr. Banker, a refined woman in her late thirties known for her sharp features and tailored business attire. Dr. Banker was the head of Anya's Viral Genesis Lab in New York.

Dr. Banker informed Anya, "We're down to five scientists. Results are slow, but we're exploring other avenues. When do you plan to visit New York?"

Anya: "I can't give you a definite time until I assess the lab after the hurricane. We'll be leaving here in two days."

***

Giddy yet exhausted, Shelley wondered aloud, "Should we make him bigger?"

It was three in the morning, and they were still working on Lance. Maya, looking weary, chuckled softly and replied, "Shh, Shelley, everyone is sleeping."

Shelley couldn't help but laugh, sinking to the floor. "Sorry, I can't help it. I'm just so tired," she whispered, stifling her laughter.

Maya adjusted Lance's briefs, concealing his anatomically correct genitals after conducting responsiveness testing.

Shelley crawled away, her laughter echoing softly until she reached the stairs and gripped the railing.

"I'm heading upstairs to pack for our morning departure. See you at breakfast, goodnight," Shelley announced, blowing a kiss to Maya.

"I'm coming up too," Maya answered. She glanced at the handsome android, Lance, and added, "You're perfect just the way you are. See you in the morning, sweetie."

"Goodnight, Maya. I'll see you in the morning, sweetheart." Lance replied.

Maya turned off the lights, plunging the living room into soft darkness. Lance, adhering to his recent directive to stand vigil, took one steady step toward the staircase to follow her.

"Ah-ah-ah," Maya whispered, stopping at the first step.

"That's not necessary, Lance. You guarded my sleep all night. Now rest." She walked back and gently guided his shoulder, turning him away from the stairs. "I know you're programmed to protect, but you need to conserve energy."

She led him to the armchair near the now-darkened television. He lowered his tall frame, his optical sensors dimming slightly as he entered low-power mode.

"Thank you," Maya said, her voice soft with affection, and she placed her hand briefly on his cheek. She started up the stairs, leaving the android sitting alone, a silent, perfect sentinel in the dark living room. Lance remained motionless, his programming for vigilance humming softly as a snore, waiting for the first sound of a command.

Chapter 11

# Goodbye

"The past is never dead. It's not even past."
- *William Faulkner.*

Shared weariness hung in the air the morning after. Everyone had prepared to return home and assess the damage, exchanging quiet greetings as they descended the stairs.

Lance, following instructions from shared files, helped Max prepare a simple breakfast. Kit, the Lee family kitchen unit, efficiently cleared the dishes once they finished eating.

I wonder if the power has returned," Shelley mused, breaking off a piece of Maya's toast and savoring the cinnamon sugar.

Maya asked, "Lance, can you give us a brief update on the situation at home?"

Lance replied, "There are no immediate alerts. Some areas are experiencing power outages, but most roads are open. You can download a detailed list of closures."

"Okay, Lance, please share that data with me now."

After breakfast, a knock on the bedroom door interrupted Anya as she packed her bag.

"You look ready to go," said Anya, her gaze settling on the doctor's new emerald green shoes. "Those pumps are lovely, and they match your blouse perfectly."

Dr. Dee smiled, "Oh, you like them? Thank you. I made them using the ShoeDye 26 unit," she replied.

"Nice, are you leaving now?"

"Yes, but I'll make a quick stop at a store before heading home. I'll be in the lab soon after."

"I'm doing the same," Anya said as she folded her clothes and placed them in her suitcase. "I wonder if we have power at the lab?"

"Thanks again for everything, Anya. I'm going to say goodbye to everyone and head out."

"I'm glad you came. I feel good about those new scientific methods; I'll send them to Dr. Banker."

Dr. Dee winked and said, "Got it. See you later. Bye." The scientist rolled her two large suitcases down the hall.

Anya wondered aloud, "Which of Dr. Dee's home units are large enough to produce luggage of that size?"

Max replied, "That would be the TrashGo unit."

"Thank you, Max."

Knowing Max's tendency to elaborate, Anya quickly added, "Max, please check the bathroom for my things and bring them to me so I can pack." As Max turned toward the bathroom, he continued: "It can also produce shelves and cabinets."

Anya laughed, "Stop," she said, knowing that his literalness could be amusing.

Mrs. Evans called out from the doorway to the bedroom, "Hello, Anya."

"Hi, Sandy. What are your plans?"

"I'm leaving now. I packed last night; my bag is by the door. Thank you for having me here."

"You're welcome."

After Mrs. Evans left, Anya noticed that Max was standing still in the bathroom and realized she had commanded him to stop. "Max," she said, "please finish checking the bathroom, pack my things, take the luggage to Carl-23, then wait for me in the living room."

Max replied, "I'm on it. Would you like to learn more about the TrashGo unit?"

Anya rolled her eyes, "No, thanks."

"You're welcome," came Max's reply.

***

Mrs. Evans and Dr. Dee left while Shelley waited in Maya's car. Anya and Maya stood at the front door, taking one last look inside. Anya hugged Maya tightly before heading to her car.

Maya closed the door, wiped her eyes, and whispered, "Goodbye, Mom and Dad."

Chapter 12

# Eye Scanner

"The eye sees only what the mind is prepared to comprehend." - *Henri Bergson.*

As Carl-23 drove midway back home, Anya noticed a grocery store. She spotted Dr. Dee and Mrs. Evans parked cars and saw Mrs. Evans go inside. Anya relaxed into her seat, deciding against stopping; chatting with them could delay her return.

"Max."

"Yes, Anya?"

"Do we need anything for the house?"

"I have a list of nine items. Shall I read it to you?"

"No, please transfer the list to Carl-23."

"Sent."

"Carl-23, find an open store on our route that carries all the items on the list."

After several miles, Carl-23 announced, "We have arrived."

Anya remained in the car, going over her notes. She glanced out the window and saw Max enter the market, followed by three other androids. At the same time, another android was leaving the store.

Anya shuffled through her papers, realizing that some pages were missing. Moments later, Max approached, and the trunk of Carl-23 opened. Max loaded the groceries and took a seat in the passenger side. Carl-23 started the engine, and Anya held out her papers to Max.

"Max, please scan these documents and let me know if any pages are missing."

Max took the documents from her hand and scanned them optically. He returned the papers and confirmed that three pages were missing.

"That's what I suspected. Fortunately, Sandy has her notes. She should be out of the store; I'll call her now."

"Hi, Sandy. Do you have a moment?"

"Yes."

"I'm missing three pages of my notes. Could they be mixed in with yours? Could you please check?"

"Yes, I'll call you back."

"Thanks."

Anya called Maya. "Hey Maya, I'm missing some notes. Could you check yours for me?"

"Sure, I'll look for them and call you back."

Maya handed her documents to Lance and said, "Lance, I need your help."

Lance nodded, "Of course, Maya. What do you need?"

"Scan these for any handwriting that isn't mine."

Lance quickly examined the stack of papers. "No, these are all your notes."

"Okay, thanks, Lance." She updated Anya with the information.

"Damn! Thanks, Maya. See you later. Oh, Sandy's calling back. Bye."

"Bye."

"I can't find my notes," informed Mrs. Evans. "I know they're around here somewhere. I'll search again. I'm heading to the lab now; I'll copy mine and have them ready when you arrive."

Anya kept her voice calm, trusting Mrs. Evans to manage the situation.

***

Immediately after the call, Mrs. Evans dropped off her groceries at home. She found her notes in Eddie's trunk and drove straight to the lab to make copies.

Chapter 13

# Dark Smoke

"Though she be but little, she is fierce." - *William Shakespeare.*

Anya glanced out of the car window, catching her breath as she took in the familiar landscape, now scarred and battered. Power lines dangled, and uprooted trees lay scattered. However, robotic workers were clearing the roads.

Carl-23 coasted to the curb, and Anya hurried toward the house. Its sensors recognized her, and the door slid open automatically. She dashed to the bathroom, feeling a wave of relief after the long journey.

Meanwhile, Max unloaded the trunk with precision, and Carl-23 glided to its designated parking spot. Max pressed buttons on the kitchen wall to open hidden compartments, and the android began pouring liquids, gels, and powders into their designated containers.

Anya bounded down the steps, passing Max in a blur as he headed upstairs. "Great! We have power here," she called over her shoulder. "Summon Carl-23. I'm heading to work now. Cancel my lunch and dinner plans; I'll be working late. Bye."

Max replied, "Got it. Bye."

Anya rushed out of the house just as Maya's car pulled up.

"I can't talk, Maya, I'm off to work. I've canceled my meals. Let me know if you want to join me for dinner elsewhere."

"Sounds good, Auntie. Bye!"

As she rode, Anya reviewed her notes. Looking out the car window, she noticed more storm damage in the area and wondered, *Do we have power at the lab?*

***

*At the lab*—A wave of unease tightened her stomach as she stepped into the building. The power had gone out, and the entry door gaped wide open. The halls were silent and eerie, with most lab rooms still closed. The absence of moving robots struck her as strange. A dark tendril of smoke curled from beneath one of the lab rooms, a sinister omen.

Anya sprinted to the door and entered, finding a corner of the lab filled with thick black smoke and fire. Through the flames and haze, she spotted the lower limbs of three figures sprawled behind the benches.

Anya dropped to her hands and knees, crawling forward as she shouted, "I'm coming! If you can hear me, say something!"

She pressed the emergency button on her phone three times.

A woman's voice responded, "Police or fire?"

"Both," Anya yelled into the phone. "Hurry! The lab's on fire. There are people on the floor who are not responding."

"We have located your position. Stay away from the fire and evacuate the building. Help is on the way," the voice assured her.

"Please hurry!" Anya coughed violently.

She ignored the dispatcher and moved through the thick smoke. Coughing while crawling, she spotted a flicker of movement nearby, the faint outline of a person. A sudden sharp blow to the back of her head sent her crashing to the floor. Just before darkness claimed her, she caught a glimpse of a dark silhouette fleeing the lab.

"Hello? Hello? Don't hang up, help is coming. Hello?" the dispatcher's voice crackled through the connected line.

Anya's eyes fluttered open, accompanied by a throbbing headache and the sensation of being dragged across the floor. Panic surged as she struggled against the two figures pulling her.

"Anya, Anya, stop! The lab's on fire. We're trying to get you out," a voice shouted.

In an instant, her temporary amnesia vanished. Andrew's loving gaze, her sister's tragedy, her brother's untimely death, and her childhood grief all rushed back to her in a painful wave. Deeply buried emotions erupted. She screamed, thrashing wildly against her rescuers.

Looking up, Anya saw Dr. Croft's eyes bulge with terror as she stared down at her. Beside Dr. Croft, Dr. Dee, identifiable by her emerald-green shoes, was pulling at Anya's lower body to drag her to safety. The smoke was thick around them.

"Step aside," a FireBot unit's voice boomed.

The three women sat against the hallway wall, gasping and coughing. A MedicAI unit, a specialized healthcare android with a smooth, neutral chassis and multiple monitoring sensors, approached them and dispensed three oxygen masks. Dr. Croft placed one on Anya, observing as FireBots and MedicAIs flooded the hallway. The MedicAI scanned them and identified Anya as the most injured.

The unit transformed, extending two arms to lift and stabilize Anya as its lower section reconfigured into a wheeled stretcher. The arms lowered her onto a comfortable surface, similar to a memory foam-lined cradle. Dr. Croft and Dr. Dee followed as the MedicAI rolled Anya toward the waiting ambulance. More MedicAIs and FireBots entered the building.

Meanwhile, Anya's LabAI units rushed past her, evacuating the structure and awaiting instructions outside at a safe distance.

Chapter 14

# Comatose

"Grief can be the garden of compassion. If you keep your heart open through everything, your pain can become your greatest ally in your life's walk." - *Rumi.*

Anya awoke in a hospital room surrounded by household plants, a blooming Peace Lily, a tall snake plant, and trailing Spider plants, softening the sterile environment. The room featured elegant early 20th-century décor, and a wall projection showcased vibrant ocean life.

Anya coughed, prompting the MedicAI unit beside her to ask in a synthesized voice, "How are you feeling?"

"I'm fine. Can I leave?"

The MedicAI responded, "You can leave in thirty-seven minutes."

Anya glanced at her arm and noticed a white strip covering her skin, dotted with small colored lights. Only a steady green light indicates that the process is complete.

Anya heard a knock and called out, "Come in."

A uniformed officer walked into the room, a woman in her mid-thirties with a short crew cut and a warm smile.

"Dr. Peters?" she asked.

"Yes."

"Hello, I'm Police Officer Stanley. How are you feeling?"

"I'm fine. Can you tell me what happened?"

"An investigation is underway. We will send a TrackAI unit to collect your statement and information."

Anya asked, "Can you tell me who was in the building?"

Officer Stanley took a notepad from her pocket. "There were six people," she said. "Dr. Croft and Dr. Dee rescued you from the fire. Dr. Blaney, Dr. Daily, and Mrs. Evans are also in the hospital."

"Oh my God! Are they okay?"

"I'm sorry, I don't have that information right now. TrackAI will be with you before you leave, and I will contact you when we know more." Officer Stanley exited the room just as Maya was entering with tears in her eyes. She hugged Anya tightly and asked, "Are you okay?"

Maya pulled back from Anya, who reassured her, "I feel fine; they're just finishing my tests."

Maya accidentally triggered the MedicAI alert, which issued a warning: "Caution! Do not remove the strip."

Shaken, Maya asked, "What happened?"

"I don't know. When I arrived at the lab, I saw a fire in the corner. I think I saw three people lying on the floor. I tried to reach them, but someone hit me on the back of the head."

The MedicAI unit swiveled its camera and said, "Please turn your head away from the camera." Anya complied, and the unit scanned the back of her head. "There is a lump consistent with a twenty percent impact, likely caused by a microscope. We will record this injury and send it to the TrackAI police station."

Anya asked her niece, "Maya, I need you to check on Dr. Blaney, Dr. Daily, and Mrs. Evans. Find out where they are and how they're doing."

"Okay, I'm on it," Maya replied as she left the room.

Dr. Guild, a pregnant woman with a gentle and professional demeanor, entered the room. She introduced herself, saying to Anya, "Dr. Peters, your lungs are clear, but we need to monitor your head injury. Please report any issues to MedicAI. Is someone staying with you?"

"Yes, my niece Maya."

The doctor continued: "You require twenty-four-hour observation, so please take it easy for now. I shouldn't need to see you again today."

Anya asked the doctor about her pregnancy, "When is your due date?"

Dr. Guild placed a hand on her belly and replied, "In two months." The doctor continued, "What do you do, Anya?" After Anya explained her job, the doctor leaned close to Anya to say, "When the Y-Plague began, things seemed hopeless for men. My husband, John, and I hadn't planned on having children because of our busy schedules. He programmed AI vehicles and customized models that sold out before construction even began. When we heard about the decline in the male population, we changed our approach. We attempted male sperm selection at the MicroSort clinic, but it failed. Then, I became pregnant naturally." Dr. Guild paused to catch her breath. "Fortunately, it's a girl. I'm naming her Johnnie after her father." Her voice trembled, and Anya could sense her struggle to hold back tears.

Maya re-entered the room where the doctor was waiting. Dr. Guild smiled at her, "Please monitor Anya for the next twenty-four hours."

Maya's expression looked concerned as she replied, "Okay." After Dr. Guild left, Maya turned to Anya and said, "I'm sorry, Aunt Anya." Her voice trembled as she continued, "Chemical asphyxiation caused the deaths of both Dr. Blaney and Dr. Daily. Mrs. Evans is on the fourth floor; she's in a coma, and it doesn't look good."

Gasping, Anya swung her legs off the bed. The MedicAI cautioned, "Please don't move until I remove the strip."

Ignoring the warning, Anya peeled off the strip and slapped it onto the MedicAI's forehead. "Let's go, Maya. Take me to Sandy."

***

They found Mrs. Evans' hospital room, which was similarly furnished and had a wall screen displaying stunning landscapes. Anya whispered, with tears welling in her eyes, "Sandy, oh Sandy, what happened?"

Maya placed a comforting hand on Anya's shoulder. Just then, a four-foot mobile data collection robot, TrackAI unit 1296, with a sleek metallic shell and integrated camera lenses, rolled into the room. In a synthesized voice, it announced: "My search indicates that Dr. Anya Peters is present. I am TrackAI unit 1296, and I am here to ask you questions."

Anya replied, "TrackAI unit, I will speak to you after I talk to my friend."

The unit responded, "Standing by."

"Maya, please go to Liz's daughters. I don't want them to hear the news from strangers or robots. Be there for them and give them a tight hug. I'll tell them myself. I'll join you shortly after I talk to this unit."

After Maya left, Anya turned to Mrs. Evans. "My dear friend, you've been like a mother to me, always strong in difficult times. I know you can get through this.

After a moment, Anya released Mrs. Evans's hand and turned to the TrackAI, recounting her arrival and the lab attack. The unit asked, "How many people in the lab were on the floor?"

"Three that I saw. It was hard to see clearly with the smoke and fire."

"Emergency dispatch and MedicAI units have confirmed your call regarding the head injury. We appreciate your cooperation. We will be in touch with you. Please verify the information displayed on this unit's screen." A display of her driver's license appeared with "Next" and "Edit" options. Anya selected "Next." The screen displayed her statement. Instead of waiting for the unit to print it out, Anya chose "Send," instantly transmitting the data stream to Max back at the house.

Chapter 15

# Orphans

"A mother's love is a song that never ends." - *Unknown.*

After leaving the hospital, Anya quickly stopped at Mrs. Evans's house before heading to Liz's home. She entered the passcode that Mrs. Evans had given her two years ago. A wave of sadness washed over Anya as she thought of Sandy's deceased husband, Barney. He resembled Barney Rubble from *The Flintstones*, with his boxy build, thick neck, short limbs, full blond hair, and small eyes. Anya had always adored Barney; he was a jolly, humorous man whom everyone loved. As she opened the door, an energetic and friendly Dachshund bounded out to greet her.

"Hello, Peanut. I see that your pet sitter brought you home. Your mom will be back soon. Where's your brother, Alley Cat?"

Anya gathered their food, bedding, and grooming supplies and placed them in Carl-23's trunk. Alley Cat, a tabby-Manx mix with orange stripes and a tailless body, entered the carrier without hesitation. The ever-joyful Peanut was more challenging to leash. The dog kept circling Anya's ankles, but Anya eventually succeeded. Finally, she covered Pretty Boy's cage with a cloth to calm the parakeet's fluttering and took them back to her place, Max waiting at the front door.

"Max, please download all caretaking and teaching protocols for a three-year-old Dachshund, an unknown-aged cat, a parakeet, and two children: seven-year-old Cindy and four-year-old Lynn. Clear out Andrew's and my office, box our documents, and contact StorageBots to convert the rooms into bedrooms for the girls. Also, please interface with Carl-23 at six in the morning; have the car transport you and the animals to the Blaney house."

"Acknowledged."

After instructing Max, Anya hurried to Carl-23, selected Liz's address, and called Maya as the car pulled away from the curb.

"Hi, Maya. How's it going?"

"The girls just got dropped off by the school bus after their play day at the park, and the TrackAI arrived about ten minutes ago."

"Do the girls know?"

"No, I told the unit to wait outside."

"Good, I'll be there in three minutes."

Maya added, "I'm playing a game with them."

"Have they asked why you are there visiting?"

Maya walked away from the girls who played with toys on the floor. She whispered, "No, I told them we were going out to dinner. They were excited to hear that their godmother is coming too."

***

Anya and Liz's friendship dated back to their college days. Anya was a bridesmaid at Liz's marriage to Richard Blaney. Liz and Richard had immediately connected with Anya and Andrew, trusting them to love and care for their daughters. Neither Liz nor Richard had any living relatives. Liz's adopted parents had been unhappy with each other, and her adopted mother died young. In contrast, Richard's adopted parents provided him with a stable, loving home. Their mutual trust in Anya was unwavering. Later, Anya and Andrew became the godparents of Liz and Richard's daughters.

***

At Dr. Blaney's home, Lynn bounced up and down with excitement as soon as Anya arrived. "Hi, Aunt Anya. Maya is here, and she said we're all going out for dinner."

Anya offered a brave smile in response. "Hello, Lynn. I think that sounds lovely."

However, seven-year-old Cindy looked at Anya suspiciously, "Aunt Anya, why is there a TrackAI waiting outside?"

Anya felt a sense of relief when she heard Cindy speak; it had been a long time since she had heard her voice following her father's death. Anya responded, "I'll find out in a minute."

Fortunately, Max sent Anya instructions on how to break the news of their mother's death to the girls. Anya walked over to the sofa and sat down, gesturing for the girls to join her. Maya watched closely as Lynn eagerly nestled up against Anya, while Cindy hesitantly made her way over to sit beside them.

"Sweethearts, I have something sad to tell you," Anya said, keeping her voice steady despite the effort it took. "Your mommy died." She paused, letting the finality of those words sink in. Her throat tightened, and tears filled her eyes as she continued: "She won't be coming home."

The words struck all at once.

Cindy and Lynn cried out together. A sharp scream, raw, broken sound torn from deep in their chests, as if neither of them had been able to stop it in time. The room felt suddenly too small, the air too thin.

For a moment, neither girl moved. Cindy's hands clenched into fists at her sides, her face pale and rigid, as though she were trying to force the meaning of the words to make sense.

Lynn shook her head slowly, as if refusing to hear them at all.

"But … how?" Cindy whispered at last, her voice trembling. "How did Mommy die?"

Lynn swallowed hard, her jaw tight. "Was she scared?" she asked, the question coming out sharper than she meant. "Did it hurt?"

Neither girl seemed ready for the answers, yet both waited, bracing themselves, trying to take in a truth that felt far too big for them.

Then the dam broke.

Cindy jumped up and dashed to her room, slamming the door behind her. Lynn looked up at Anya, her eyes filled with questions, soon welling up with tears. She wrapped her arms around Anya's waist, holding on tightly as she sobbed loudly, "Mommy, I want my mommy!"

Anya's heart clenched. She knelt and gathered Lynn into her arms, holding her close as the child's sobs shook her small body. She pressed her cheek against Lynn's hair, rocking her gently, wishing she could give her the one thing she was asking for.

"I know," Anya whispered, her own voice breaking. "I know, sweetheart."

From down the hall came the muffled sound of Cindy crying. Angry, sharp sobs that rose and fell behind the closed door. Anya glanced toward the hallway, torn between the two girls, knowing Cindy needed her, too.

Anya tightened her hold on Lynn, breathing slowly, steadily, trying to be an anchor in a moment when everything felt like it was drifting apart.

Maya gazed at Anya and asked, "Should I go check on Cindy?"

"Wait a moment; give her time to mourn."

Chapter 16

# The Girls

"Hope and fear are two sides of the same coin."

- *Robert Louis Stevenson.*

Maya knelt beside the couch and hugged Lynn, who was crying and shouting, "I want my mommy! Where is she? I want her home, Mommy!"

After half an hour, exhausted, Lynn rested her head on Maya's lap and fell asleep.

Meanwhile, Anya got up and walked to Cindy's door, leaning her head against it. She could hear Cindy's muffled sobs. Anya tapped gently, but there was no response. Slowly, she opened the door and found Cindy crying in bed. Anya sat on the edge of the mattress.

Cindy turned and hugged Anya tightly, and they both cried together. After a moment, Cindy lifted her head, looked into Anya's eyes, and asked, "Where's Mommy?"

"Your Mommy passed away, my sweet girl. Her body stopped working, and now she is gone."

"Can we go and get her?"

"Oh, honey, no. Once a person dies, their body can't come back. We can't go and get her, but we can keep her in our hearts forever."

After about an hour, Anya quietly left Cindy sleeping. She found Maya on the couch, still asleep, with Lynn resting on her lap. Anya stepped outside to the TrackAI 924 unit. As she approached, the hibernating unit sensed her presence and activated.

"Dr. Anya Peters, are the occupants of this home available for a report?"

"I am here; I have delivered the report."

The unit displayed the report, Anya signed, and the unit uploaded the information to headquarters and sent a copy to Max.

That evening, the women had dinner, but the girls did not eat. The atmosphere was solemn. The girls cried and slept restlessly throughout the night. Anya slept in Cindy's room on the single bed, holding her close and stroking her hair, while Maya did the same in Lynn's room.

***

In the morning, Max arrived with the animals and began preparing breakfast. Anya woke up to find Cindy still asleep beside her. Maya entered from the adjoining girls' rooms, picked up a doll off the floor, and placed it on the nightstand. She whispered, "Lynn is still sleeping. What's the plan?"

"I'm not hungry, I'm heading to the lab and the police station to find out what happened."

Maya said, "I'll stay here. I've contacted Shelley to come over with Lance. We can conduct the testing and programming here."

"Alright, we'll bring the girls to my house tonight, also, "Max, please photograph their rooms. Contact the paint store and instruct the PaintBots to match Cindy's colors for Andrew's office and Lynn's colors for mine."

"Understood," Max replied.

Max walked past Lynn on his way to her room. Lynn, wearing a long nightgown, rubbed her eyes and asked, "Aunt Anya, do I have to go to school now?" As she spoke, she noticed the animals in the house. Squealing with excitement, Lynn ran over to Peanut, picked him up, and lifted the small dog into her arms.

Anya greeted Lynn with a smile, saying, "Hello. No, you don't have to go to school, but it is breakfast time."

Lynn, feeling hungry, set Peanut down on the floor, climbed onto a kitchen chair, and watched Max as he prepared her breakfast. She picked up a slice of toast and asked, "Is Mommy eating breakfast too?"

Anya and Maya exchanged a sorrowful glance.

Maya said, "I'll talk to her again."

Just as Anya reached the front door, Cindy, still in her pajamas, burst out of her room. She screamed and ran to Anya, wrapping her arms tightly around her waist. Tears streamed down her face as she cried, "No, don't leave … I don't want you to go—I don't want you to die, too!"

Anya knelt to face Cindy. "Honey, Maya is here, and I'll be back soon. We're going to have a wonderful dinner, and you can sleep at my house tonight."

Sniffling, Cindy noticed the animals and asked, "Are they yours, Aunt Anya?"

Anya smiled, "I'm just temporarily caring for them. I'll be back later. Maya is having Shelley come over; do you remember Shelley? She will be here with a surprise."

"I remember Shelley." Lynn shouted from the kitchen. She quickly spooned food into her mouth, swallowed without chewing, and asked, "Can I have a surprise, too?"

"Yes," Anya replied.

She turned her gaze back to Cindy and asked, "Would you like to meet Lance?"

Cindy clung to Anya's neck, refusing to let go. "No…I don't want you to go!" she cried.

Maya called out, "Cindy, please come here, sweetheart. It's time to eat your breakfast before Shelley and Lance arrive."

"Lance? Who is Lance?" Lynn asked, curious.

But Cindy, tears streaming down her face, shouted, "I want Mommy home!" She turned and ran back to her room, slamming the door behind her.

Lynn's expression changed when she saw her sister rush to her room. Tears welled up in her eyes as she looked at Anya. Lynn yelled, "I want Mommy too!" She leapt off her seat and ran to her room, slamming the door behind her.

Chapter 17

# We're All Going to Die!

"Grief can be the garden of sympathy." - *George Eliot.*

Anya made her way to Carl-23 and informed the vehicle to take her to the hospital. Upon arriving, she quickly walked to the station desk and approached nurse unit G233. The NurseAI unit turned its head to greet her warmly.

"Welcome. How may I assist you?" it asked.

"Yes, Nurse Unit, could you provide me with information about Mrs. Sandy Evans?" Anya responded.

"Sandy Evans?" the unit echoed, its synthesized voice remaining steady. "The attending doctor is Dr. Mary Guild. Would you like to send her a message?"

"Yes, please inform her that Dr. Anya Peters is requesting an update on Mrs. Sandy Evans. Here is my contact information." Anya tapped the message icon on the unit's screen, entered her details, and pressed send.

Anya hurried to her bedside and took her hand. She spoke softly, reassuringly, "Don't worry about the animals, Sandy. They are safe with me until you get better. Please heal quickly, come back to us. I'm going to the lab to assess the damage. I'm determined to find out who is responsible. When I do…"

"Dr. Peters? I'm Dr. Guild. We met yesterday. How are you doing?"

"I'm feeling better, thank you. I have a mild headache, but overall, I feel much better."

"Are you related to Mrs. Evans?"

"Only through work and friendship. Mrs. Evans has no living relatives, and I'm the closest thing she has to family. Please, doctor, how is she?"

Dr. Guild stepped away from the bed, her expression serious. "I'm sorry, Dr. Peters. If she comes out of this coma, it will truly be a miracle. The team filtered her blood and cleared her lungs of smoke, but she suffered severe head trauma. MedicAI reported that a medical instrument may have caused the injury. The impact was ten times more intense than what happened to you."

"Is there any brain activity?" Anya whispered.

"It's barely there, significantly reduced, and remaining below the level of consciousness. I see you left your contact number. I'll reach out as soon as Mrs. Evans's condition changes."

"Thank you, Doctor Guild."

As she left the hospital, Anya called Dr. Croft. The scientist's voice filled with genuine concern. "Anya, how are you doing?"

"I'm out of the hospital and feeling fine. How about you? Were you hurt?"

"No, I'm fine. I'm heading to the lab now. How are the doctors and Mrs. Evans?"

Anya sighed. "Both doctors died from chemical asphyxiation, and Sandy…Mrs. Evans is in a coma."

A moment of silence passed between them. Dr. Croft gently said, "Oh, Anya, I'm so sorry," and added, "How can I help?"

"Do you know who's back in town?"

"No."

"Could you please call everyone from both teams and ask them to meet me at the lab? I would prefer not to mention the women; I'll handle that myself. I'm going to the lab to assess the damage and get the LabAIs back up and running. I need to access the data. I'll also call Dr. Dee to check on her. Thank you, Jean, for pulling me out and saving my life."

"Fortunately, Dr. Dee and I were there. We found you on the floor. I'm sorry that the smoke was too thick to search for anyone else. We only managed to pull you out."

"Did you see anyone else in the building?"

"No, I just arrived and saw Dr. Dee running towards me, shouting that the lab was on fire."

"Jean, I have Liz's girls."

Dr. Croft sighed, "Call me if you need anything at all, Anya."

Anya knew that Dr. Croft understood loss. She had recently taken in her nine-year-old cousin, Julie. Julie's mother had struggled with postpartum depression and bipolar disorder, tragically ending her life by suicide when Julie was seven. Julie's father succumbed to the Y-Plague, leaving Dr. Croft to become an instant mother.

"Anya, have you heard from Dr. Dee since the fire? I've tried reaching her several times."

"Me too; I called a few times, but there was no answer. I will try again after I stop by Dr. Daily's house to inform her sister, Mandy, about the bad news."

***

*At Dr. Linda Daily's home*—When Mandy, Dr. Daily's sister, opened the door, a flicker of recognition appeared in her eyes. "Linda's not here," she told Anya. "She left for work yesterday, and I don't know why she hasn't come home. Do you know where she is?"

"Yes, hello, Mandy. May I come in?" Anya asked. Mandy pushed the screen door wide open, allowing Anya to step inside. Anya followed Mandy into the kitchen.

Mandy, a disheveled sixty-year-old woman, wore a stained housedress, and her white hair was a frizzy mess. She asked Anya, "Would you like some coffee, tea, or anything else?"

Anya noticed a small, white, fluffy poodle sleeping on the kitchen floor. "No, thank you."

"You remember Gigi, my dog?" Mandy asked and staggered towards the cupboard. She grabbed a new bottle of vodka and poured a generous amount into her cup. "Oh, would you like a drink? Sit down, sit down," she repeated, gesturing to Anya.

"No, thank you; Mandy, this is hard for me to say…"

Mandy slurred, "What's going on?" as she spilled vodka on the linoleum floor.

"Mandy, I'm so sorry. Your sister, Linda, died in a fire at the lab yesterday."

Mandy's expression went blank. Her body froze in place like a statue, holding a tilted cup dripping vodka onto the floor.

"Mandy?" Anya asked, unsure if she had heard her.

Mandy spun around, vodka splashing from her cup, and shouted at Anya, "Oh my God, look what you made me do!"

Anya realized that trying to talk to Mandy in her drunken state would be futile.

Mandy yelled, "Who cares?" Her voice filled with desperation. "I don't care!"

Anya understood Mandy's intoxication when she noticed the poodle, Gigi, trying to stand but tumbled into a tipsy slumber instead.

"Linda should be home soon," Mandy mumbled, but the reality of Anya's words seemed lost on her.

"It was nice seeing you, Mandy, but I have to go."

"Why don't you stay until Linda gets home?" Mandy pleaded, following Anya toward the front door.

As Anya stepped onto the porch, Mandy called out, "I'll tell Linda you were here. She'll be sorry she missed you."

A wave of despair washed over Anya. Mandy's decline was heart-wrenching; she had turned to drinking after her minister husband, Brad, died from the Y-Plague. Following his death, Mandy moved in with her sister. Although Dr. Daily had talked about Mandy's drinking, Anya hadn't realized the severity of the situation until now.

As Anya began to drive away, Mandy shouted, "We're all going to die!"

Chapter 18

# The Weight of Grief

"Hope is being able to see that there is light despite all of the darkness." - *Desmond Tutu.*

On the road, Anya commanded Carl-23 to pull over. In the back seat, Anya curled into a fetal position as tears finally broke free. Mandy's warning echoed in her mind: "We're all going to die!" Anya screamed, "I can't do this anymore!" Tissues emerged from a compartment beneath the seat, filling the air with a hint of jasmine. Anya took a few and, in a whisper, said, "Thank you."

She sat up and gazed at the city skyline. The devastation caused by the hurricane was stark against the urban landscape. Groups of women and MedicAI volunteers were pulling sheet-covered bodies from homes, while freshly dug burial plots dotted the area. Yet, in nearby regions, life thrived; robots transformed barren lots into productive edible gardens, offering a fragile, green reminder of her childhood Garden of Eden project.

From a distance, Anya admired the lush greenery. She often found peace here after work, watching the sunset and observing the transformation of barren lots into sustainable gardens over the past twenty years. However, today she felt a deep sadness, her heart heavy with the loss of her friends and the partial destruction of what had once seemed like a miracle. "Take me to work," she said.

The car moved ahead as Anya's thoughts shifted to Cindy and Lynn. What future awaited them on a planet without men? While the androids were excellent caretakers and teachers, they could never replace the nurturing love that their parents had provided. Anya shifted her focus to her immediate concerns: evaluating the damage, restoring the facility, and continuing their work in the lab.

Carl-23 arrived at the lab building just as Anya's watch signaled a call from Dr. Croft.

"Hello?"

"Anya?"

"Hi, Jean."

"We just received a call from Mandy asking for her sister."

Anya sighed and explained Mandy's condition to Dr. Croft.

"I'm so sorry, Anya. What are you going to do?"

"I'll call TrackAI to dispatch help to her home."

***

*The Last Male*—Hospitals around the world raced to save the last male of the human species. Cincinnati Children's Hospital prepared for Malia Akana, an eight-month pregnant Hawaiian resident. Malia, isolated to deliver a healthy, tiny infant named Keoki. The world watched and prayed for the newborn's survival.

The infant Keoki bravely battled the disease moment by moment, but the relentless viral assault weakened him. Ultimately, Keoki succumbed to the Y-Plague. The tragic extinction of the entire gender plunged the world into profound despair and grief, altering the course of humanity's future.

***

Anya called out, "TV, off." The screen in the lounge area of her lab building went black. Wiping her eyes, Anya faced her two teams. "I understand if no one wants to be here. If you wish to leave, I will completely understand. However, I have more unfortunate news to share." She paused, clearing her throat as tears welled in her eyes, again. "Dr. Daily and Dr. Blaney died in the fire from chemical asphyxiation, and someone attacked Mrs. Evans; she is currently in a coma at the hospital."

The room fell silent as shock washed over the women. Dr. Gleeson's knees buckled, her eyes shut, and she went down hard. The others rushed to help her.

Dr. Croft supported Dr. Gleeson, and asked, "What do you want us to do?"

"I'm not sure yet," Anya responded, noticing a bandage on Dr. Crofts' right forearm. "What happened to your arm?"

"I splashed boiling water while rushing to make breakfast," the scientist explained.

Anya continued, "The police are investigating the lab and may question us. We need to wait for their inspection. Dr. Croft or I will contact you when we can assess the damage."

Once the women left the building, Dr. Croft asked Anya, "Were you able to reach Dr. Dee? I've left her messages, but I haven't received a response."

"No, there's no answer. I'll try again later." Anya noticed a large bruise on the back of Dr. Croft's upper arm, "That's quite a bruise you have there, Jean."

"What bruise?" the scientist asked, confused.

"The one on your right upper arm," Anya clarified.

Dr. Croft lifted her arm to take a look and responded, "Wow ... Where did that come from?" After thinking for a moment, she added, "It must have happened while I was pulling you out of the lab. Now that I think about it,

I vaguely remember bumping into something, maybe the lab bench."

Before leaving the building, Anya and Dr. Croft glanced into the lab room and observed the TrackAI forensics units hard at work.

"Anya, I don't think we can use this lab anymore; the smell is overwhelming throughout the building. Do you have any suggestions?

"See if you can find us another lab facility. Have you seen our LabAI units?"

"Yes, I stored them in room two. I didn't see or find any damage to them. What do you want to do with them?"

"Leave them here until we find a new place. I'll stop by Dr. Dee's house and head over to the hospital to see Mrs. Evans again."

Dr. Croft responded, "Okay, I'll check in with you when I find a new lab facility."

As Anya left the building, she ordered Carl-23 to take her to Dr. Dee's house while she called Maya.

Chapter 19

# The Unanswered Call

"The silence of a friend is a terrible thing." - *Russian Proverb.*

Through her holographic watch, Anya noticed that Maya had been crying. Concerned, Anya asked, "Maya, are you okay?"

Maya replied, "Shelley and I have been crying non-stop over Keoki's death. The girls are in Cindy's room. I offered to take them to the park with Max and me, but they won't stop crying or come out."

"They didn't watch the news … did they?"

"No, they don't know anything about it. What should I do?"

"Nothing, just let them cry and sleep. I'll be back after I check on a few things."

"Okay."

***

Anya arrived at Dr. Dee's house and rang the doorbell, but there was no answer. She knocked and called out, "Dr. Dee, hello! June?" Still no response.

She walked over to the front window and peeked inside. The kitchen light was on, and a beam of light shone from beneath the bathroom door, illuminating the hallway.

"June, it's Anya!" she shouted, but still received no answer.

Anya reached for her wristwatch to contact the TrackAI station for assistance. However, her watch indicated an incoming call from the hospital.

"Hello."

"Yes, hello, Dr. Peters, Anya, are you available to talk?" It's Dr. Guild.

"Yes, of course. How is Mrs. Evans?"

"I think you should know that Mrs. Evans is experiencing nonconvulsive status epilepticus (NCSE). Her EEG shows abnormal brainwave patterns."

Anya paced along the porch and asked, "What's next?"

Dr. Guild explained, "We could administer intravenous benzodiazepines such as lorazepam, followed by additional antiepileptic drugs (AEDs) like levetiracetam, valproate, or fosphenytoin if the initial treatment fails. However, it's important to note this treatment might not improve outcomes for an individual with brain injuries."

"Is this Sandy's first episode?" Anya inquired.

"Yes, this is her first recorded incident. How would you like me to proceed?"

Anya said, "I approve of anything that will help Sandy. Please assist her. Do I need to provide anything on my end?"

"No, this recorded communication is sufficient. We will begin immediately, and I'll call you with the results."

"Thank you, Dr. Guild. Goodbye."

Anya called the police station and asked, "Could you do a wellness check on Dr. June Dee?"

***

A TrackAI unit located Anya by her watch and arrived at her location within minutes of her call.

"Dr. Anya Peters, I am TrackAI unit number 7315. How may I assist you?"

"I have been trying to reach Dr. June Dee since yesterday."

TrackAI unit 7315 activated its infrared thermal imaging. "Non-active human signature detected in the house," it ordered. "Stand back. We must enter. Do not follow." As Anya stepped back, the unit placed its hand over the keyhole, reshaped it into a key tool, and unlocked the door. Rolling over the threshold, it stood before the bathroom door and repeated the procedure.

A MedicAI approached Anya from behind and said, "Coming through, please move aside." Curiosity got the best of her, and Anya followed. As she looked over the units, she saw Dr. Dee lying dead in a tub filled with bloody water. Shocked, Anya screamed: "Oh no!" A TrackAI blocked her from going any further. Anya shouted, "What happened?"

The TrackAI insisted that Anya leave, saying, "We need your full cooperation. You'll have to leave the premises and wait outside for a unit to take your statement."

Anya gripped her stomach, nausea rising as the room tilted. Abruptly, another unit entered the house. She stepped aside to let it pass, and as she was leaving, she noticed an envelope on a console table near the door, addressed to her. She reached out to touch it.

"Don't touch anything," a TrackAI warned. "This is a crime scene. Please exit the dwelling and wait outside."

Anya insisted, "But this envelope has my name on it."

The unit flatly said, "Follow instructions, or we will arrest you for obstruction of justice. Is that understood?"

Anya asked, "When can I have the letter meant for me?"

"Once we finish the investigation, you can contact the station for further instructions. Do you understand?"

"Yes." She knew there was nothing else she could do but follow its commands.

"A TrackAI unit, number 6224, is waiting outside for your statement. Please exit."

Anya stepped outside as another MedicAI unit entered the premises.

Anya approached the unit waiting for her and noticed a document displayed on its front screen. Below the screen, a slot opened, revealing a keypad for her to use. The screen showed her information and prompted her to either accept the details or make edits. Anya chose 'Accept' and directed the unit to "Send her a copy" before returning to her car.

Anya commanded her watch, "Call Dr. Croft."

"Calling."

Dr. Croft couldn't believe what she was hearing.

"What … Dr. Dee's dead? There was a letter? What did it say?"

"I couldn't read it, but I will contact the station once I get home. Once I have more information, I'll call you so you can reach out to everyone, including the labs in New York and Texas."

"Okay, I will talk to you later and update you on the new facility I found."

"Great."

Anya hung up with Dr. Croft and called Maya. "When I get back, I need a private moment to talk to you and Shelley, away from the girls."

"Sure," Maya said, "I'll have Max and Lance create a project for them."

"I'll be there soon. Anya leaned back in her seat and began to cry. She thought: *When will this chain of strange and catastrophic events come to an end?*

Chapter 20

# The Letter

"Grief is the last act of love we can give to those we loved. Where there is deep grief, there was great love."
- *Attributed to Annette J. Dunlea.*

Anya arrived at the Blaney home feeling composed. She greeted the children with a smile, saying, "Hello, Cindy, hello, Lynn."

Lynn raised her hands to show off a pliable, marble-colored dough and proudly announced, "Max and Lance taught us how to make homemade playdough."

Anya bent down closer. "That looks very pretty. You'll have to teach me how to make it next time. Do you know where Aunt Maya and Shelley are?"

Cindy sat in the corner of the room, petting Alley Cat, and said, "Maya is taking a shower."

Lynn, raising her voice, added, "Shelley is in the kitchen with Lance," as she pinched the dough between her fingers.

Max entered the living room and reminded Anya, "You received several reports from the police station."

Anya addressed the girls, "Please ask Lance to help you feed the animals in the kitchen. Also, let Shelley know I need to speak with her."

Alley Cat jumped off Cindy's lap when she stood up. Both girls replied, "Okay," as they walked into the kitchen.

Anya turned to Max and said, "Please print the reports for me," as they entered Liz's study together. While reading a section of the report, Anya felt a wave of dizziness. Max quickly reached out to support her and guided her to a chair.

Maya walked into the office, her hair wrapped in a towel, followed closely by Shelley. They exchanged quick smiles before noticing Anya seated in the chair, looking pale as bleached bread. With shared worried glances, Maya asked, "Aunt Anya, what's wrong?"

Anya's voice trembled as she handed them a copy of the police report. "You need to see this." The color drained from their faces as they read the report together.

Maya said, "It says Dr. June Dee committed suicide."

As they continued reading, Shelley gasped. "She … she killed them on purpose?"

Anya's voice was barely a whisper. "It seems so."

The three women stood side by side, reading a detailed letter that accompanied the report. It outlined Dr. Dee's chilling confession that reflected the mental unfolding that had overtaken her.

Maya recited Dr. Dee's confession aloud: "I didn't allow the Skypad 5 to download the results, and I don't regret sabotaging the lab and stopping the Y cure." I contaminated each result to prevent you from succeeding. I took your notes while you were in the shower because you had found a viable result. I didn't mean to hurt anyone on our team, and I wasn't aware that anyone would be in the lab so early. But when they arrived after I set the room on fire, I was trapped inside. I'm sorry, Anya; I didn't intend for you to get hurt, too. However, I'm glad our planet will no longer suffer at the hands of madmen."

Shelley exclaimed, "Wow!"

Maya asked, "What are you going to do now?"

Anya anxiously replied, "This is such a mess. The media will exploit this."

"Max, I need you to gather all the information on Dr. June Dee's history and show me her employment files."

Max connected to the printer and printed the relevant data about Dr. Dee.

"I'm hungry," Lynn said, cradling Alley Cat at the office doorway. Lynn's unexpected presence caught the women off guard.

Anya asked, "Hi, sweetie … Where's Cindy?"

"She's in her bedroom playing with Peanut and crying for Mommy. I'm hungry; when are we going to eat?"

"We're going to eat now. Let's head to the kitchen and let Cindy know we're about to eat, okay?"

"Okay," Lynn agreed, gently placing Alley Cat on the floor. She ran out of the office calling for her sister, "Cindy, we're going to eat now!"

Anya continued, "I have an idea, but let's discuss my plan after dinner."

"I'm going to finish drying my hair and join you in the dining room," Maya added.

"I'll go into the kitchen to watch Lance help out. I wonder what Kit is preparing for dinner," said Shelley.

"Shelley, please call me when everyone sits down to eat. I want some time to read the police reports," said Anya.

"Okay," Shelley replied before leaving the office.

Max walked over to Anya and placed a stack of printed papers on the desk. Thirty-five minutes later, Anya stopped reading and set the papers aside for later. Unawares, Lynn rushed in with Peanut trotting behind her, and asked, "Are you coming to dinner, Aunt Anya?"

"Yes, I'll race you," Anya answered.

Lynn giggled and took off running with Anya close behind. Anya scooped Lynn up and began tickling her. Lynn kicked and thrashed with laughter until Anya finally set her down.

***

After dinner, Max took the girls and Peanut out for a walk while Anya explained her idea to Maya and Shelley.

Maya paced the floor and asked, "Do you think this is a good idea? It's a big change, not just for us, but for the girls too."

Shelley, standing by the office doorway, replied, "I think it's a good idea. I'll go with you." She sat down, and Alley Cat jumped onto her lap. Shelley continued, "I'll let my mom know so she won't worry. Plus, it's only during the week, right?"

"I think so," Anya glanced over at Maya for input.

"I can handle it ... Shelley, you can come and go whenever you need," said Maya.

"Great! I'll join you. You know me, I'm always looking for a new adventure," Shelley responded excitedly.

"I'll call Dr. Croft, send her Dr. Dee's police report, and update her on our plans," said Anya, and picked up the stack of papers.

"Has Max discovered anything about Dr. Dee?" asked Maya, brushing her hair.

"No, I reviewed it twice, but I couldn't find anything that suggests Dr. Dee was a troubled person. However, I believe reporters will soon arrive and start hounding us about this situation."

Chapter 21

# The Journey Northeast

"Every new beginning comes from some other beginning's end." - *Seneca.*

While Max took the girls and the dog out for a walk after dinner, Maya suggested, "Should we go back to your house tonight?"

"No, I'll send Max to grab a few things from my house, and I'll let him know to be cautious of anyone following him. Maya, please make a list of things you need. Shelley, how about you?"

Shelley replied, "Nope, I'm good."

At that moment, Alley Cat jumped off Shelley's lap. The front door opened, and Cindy burst in, visibly crying. She raced to her room and shut the door. Max and Cindy guided Peanut into the house.

Lynn asked, "Can we play a game?"

"Honey, why is Cindy crying?"

"I don't know, but maybe she got sad when I told her I miss Mommy. She stopped talking and started to cry."

Anya hugged Lynn and said, "If you girls finish your homework and take a bath, and if it's not too late … we can play a game before bedtime."

"Yay! Can Peanut take a bath with me?" Peanut barked in agreement.

"Max, please prepare a bath for Lynn and Peanut together."

"Can I take a bath with Alley Cat, too?"

"Cats don't like water. Would you like Pretty Boy to be in the room with you? Maybe you can get him to sing for you while you bathe."

Lynn was thrilled with the idea; she grabbed Pretty Boy's cage and dragged it across the floor. She began to talk to him, saying, "Are you a pretty bird? Who's a pretty boy? I'm going to teach you how to sing."

Max walked over to Lynn and lifted the cage off the floor.

Lynn shouted at Max, "I can do it!"

Max replied, "Miss Lynn, we don't want Pretty Boy to get hurt, right?"

"Okay," Lynn insisted, "but when I get bigger, I want to do it myself."

Max smiled at her and said, "Of course, Miss Lynn. When you're older, you can handle it yourself.

"Also, Lance, please help Cindy with her bath after I finish talking to her."

"Yes, Anya."

Anya knocked on Cindy's door. Cindy's voice shouted, "Go away."

Anya gently called out, "Hi, honey. I want you to know that a bath is ready for you, and perhaps we can play some games afterward."

Cindy did not respond. Lance, standing next to Anya, asked, "May I help?"

Anya nodded and stepped aside to watch.

"Miss Cindy, may I come in? Pretty please, with sugar on top?"

Hearing Lance's muffled voice behind the door, Cindy replied, "Okay, Lance, you can come in, but nobody else."

Both Max and Lance served as the go-to dads. The androids fulfilled every role: caregiver, educator, nurse, friend, father, and trusted confidant.

***

The Next Morning, Anya contacted Dr. Croft to discuss her plans. Dr. Croft informed her that she had located a building just a mile away from the burned lab.

"We will move the undamaged equipment to the new location and resume our work. Did the police find any video recordings of the fire at the lab?"

"No, the police report indicates that the power in that area was out during and after the hurricane, so no recorded footage of the incident exists."

"Damn! What about the LabAIs? Did they record anything unusual?"

"No, that was strange. The police checked and reported that someone must have rolled the LabAIs into the maintenance closet after we left the building, so there was no evidence of the incident. I need to contact Dr. Banker in New York. Call me after you settle into the new lab, and I'll join you."

"I will."

After finishing all her business calls, Anya informed the girls that they would be leaving on a trip after breakfast. The girls got upset when they heard the news.

Lynn exclaimed, "But I don't want to leave. I want to see my friends at the park." She threw herself on the floor, thrashing, kicking, and screaming, "I want to see my friends Judy and Barbie at the park!"

Cindy asked, "Do we have to go, Aunt Anya?"

Once Lynn noticed no one was paying attention to her outburst, she got up off the floor and approached Anya.

"It's okay, girls, we are coming too," said Maya, nodding towards Shelley.

Still upset, Lynn screamed, "But I don't want to leave. I want to see my friends at the park!"

Shelley asked the girls, "Do you like shopping?"

"Yes," Lynn replied, while Cindy nodded in agreement.

"Okay. Let's go shopping. While we're at it, why don't we eat lunch and go to the park?"

Cindy smiled, and Lynn, who had been sniffling, said, "Can I go shopping with you, too?"

Cindy chimed in, "Me too!"

"Of course you can," Shelley replied.

Anya commanded the androids, "Max, please help Cindy get dressed and pack her luggage for the trip. Lance, please do the same for Lynn."

The girls ran into their rooms, followed closely by the androids.

Maya asked, "Aunt Anya, when do you want to leave?"

"How about we leave in half an hour? Does that work for you?"

Maya replied, "Yes, I'm ready." She turned to Shelley and asked, "What about you?"

"Yes, I can be ready."

Maya asked, "Should I help get the animals into the cars?"

Anya said, "Yes, Maya, take Lance, Shelley, Lynn, and Peanut with you. Oh, and don't forget Pretty Boy, too. I'll take Max, Cindy, and Alley Cat with me and load all their bedding and grooming supplies in Carl-23's trunk."

Forty-three minutes later, everyone was in the vehicles. Anya said, "Max, transmit the signal to Lance that we are ready for take-off."

Both car engines lit up to life as the vehicles began their transformation into aircraft. Side panels opened and rotated into wings. The crafts lifted off the ground and hovered above the road as the tires folded beneath the body. With incredible speed, they soared toward their new destination: New York.

Chapter 22

# Cora

"We must be willing to let go of the life we have planned, so as to have the life that is waiting for us." - *E.M. Forster.*

After hours of flight, the girls were acting excited. The vehicles landed in Highland Park, New York.

Anya suggested, "Let's stretch our legs. We can take a quick walk. Let the girls play in the park. Later, have lunch at the Gate House in Village Gate Square. After that, we'll hit the road—I have a meeting at three."

"Sounds good … Will Shelley and I be needed for this meeting?"

"Absolutely. We all need to be there. Let's start by showcasing Lance's upgraded improvements."

Cindy and Lynn were excited to be out of the car, and they quickly ran towards the playground, claiming the slides and swings as their own domain. Meanwhile, Anya, Maya, and Shelley used the brief break to finalize their schedules. The girls' laughter provided a cheerful backdrop to their focused discussion.

After an hour, they faced a parental dilemma: how to get the children to leave the playground. Lynn, in particular, was inconsolable after quickly forming a bond with two other girls. Tears streamed down her face as she sobbed, "I don't want to go. I want to stay here with my new friends!" Cindy found a companion, too, and her departure drew equal resistance.

"I can stay with them while you two go ahead," said Shelley. "I promised them a shopping trip. If you two want to leave now, I'll meet you at the house at two o'clock. I'm sure the girls will need a break after eating and shopping."

Anya replied, "That works for me," noticing Lynn tugging at Shelley's arm. "I'll eat at the house and prepare for the meeting."

Maya asked Shelley, "Are you okay with me going with Anya? Are you sure you can manage with the girls on your own?"

Shelley took a deep breath, her eyes welling up with tears. "Yes." She paused for a moment, adding: "I did this with my three deceased nephews."

Anya asked, "Are you sure about this, Shelley?"

"Yes, absolutely. You two go. I need this. I need to be here," Shelley replied.

Maya's eyes filled with tears. "I'll stay with you."

"No, go, I'll see you later."

Meanwhile, Anya and Maya returned to find Alley Cat perched on Max's lap in the passenger seat while Lance reappeared after walking Peanut.

Maya commanded, "Lance, take Pretty Boy and Peanut to Carl-23. We'll leave Billy here with Shelley."

Anya added, "Max, I want you to stay with Shelley and the girls."

"Understood."

After successfully loading the animals into the spacecraft Carl-23, they took off. The spacecraft landed in front of Anya's childhood home, where a beautiful robot named Cora waited. Cora, an elegant android with fair skin, dark blue eyes, and short brown hair, was dressed in a pale blue dress. She opened the front door of Barron Peters' house.

***

Barron Peters, Anya's father, founded AIRobo, Inc. and led a robotic empire that first introduced the Max and Maxi AI androids in 2031. By 2035, these androids had become ubiquitous, with billions sold worldwide.

Designed for various tasks, they significantly enhanced precision and efficiency across industries.

As the two women unloaded the animals, Maya turned to Anya and said, "I don't know about you, but I find it creepy that Grandpa has Cora looking like Grandma. What do you think?... Is Cora in the house alone?"

Anya sighed, "Yes, I know. I talked to Grandpa about it. He loved your Grandma, but his severe depression drove him to create Cora. I understand that now. He was unable to work for several years, but eventually, he started dating again. However, he didn't like any of the women he courted, and neither did we kids. One woman he dated wanted to redecorate our house after their third date. We felt relieved when your Grandpa saw through her scheme. After that, he created Cora. I was only ten at the time, and I was shocked and angry at first. I wouldn't even leave my room. When Cora came to serve me food, I threw it at her and yelled: 'I hate you! You're not my mom!' It took me a while to realize that my anger towards Cora was really about my mother's death. My brother, your uncle Greg, played lots of tricks on Cora—we all did."

Maya, clearly surprised, asked, "Mom never told me this story. What did she do to Cora?"

"Marsha, your mom regretted her rebellious acts towards Cora. But I remember this one day, your mom told Cora that she needed makeup to look pretty. Your mother put a lot of makeup on the android, and Cora ended up looking like a clown with frizzy hair. Grandpa didn't get mad because he understood what we were going through."

Anya lowered her voice and added, "Instead, Grandpa took Cora into the bathroom, washed her face, and brushed her hair. The next day, he changed Cora's eye and hair color."

"What did Uncle Greg do?"

"I'll tell you later," Anya whispered.

***

Anya turned to face Cora and said, "Hello, Cora. How is everything at the homestead?"

Cora replied, "Everything is in shipshape." Standing near Carl-23 in her pale blue dress and dark blue hair bow, she asked, "Do you need help unpacking?"

"Yes, please take Peanut and Pretty Boy inside and place them in the living room. Then, unload the trunk and bring everything else inside as well," Anya instructed.

Cora smiled and responded, "Understood."

Maya offered, "I'll bring Alley Cat inside."

"Cora, please make us lunch and prepare three bedrooms: one for Lynn, who is four years old, another for Cindy, who is seven, and the last one for Shelley, an adult. They'll be arriving around two this afternoon."

"Maya, will you be using your room?" Anya asked.

"Yes, that's fine with me, thanks."

"Would you prefer the east or west wing bedrooms for the visitors?" asked Cora.

"Please make sure all the rooms are next to ours in the east wing," Anya replied.

Cora, lifting items three times her weight, said, "Understood."

Maya directed Lance, who was seated in the Carl-23, "Lance, please meet me in Grandpa's study and prepare my papers for the meeting."

Lance noticed Cora when he exited the vehicle.

"Hello, my name is Lance."

"I'm Cora. Nice meeting you."

"Same here."

***

After lunch, they heard Billy, Maya's car land outside. Max opened the front door. Lynn's excited voice echoed through the foyer: "Wow! Is this a castle?" she shouted. Cindy, standing next to her sister, gazed upwards at the high ceiling, her expression filled with awe.

Anya, Maya, and Lance emerged from the study to greet them.

Anya said, "I would call it a house, but it is more like a mansion."

Shelley walked in with her arms full of shopping bags, and a stuffed teddy bear tumbled out of one of the bags. Cora emerged from the kitchen and picked the teddy bear from the floor. She said, "I'll take these to your rooms."

Bouncing with excitement, Lynn asked, "How many bedrooms are there? Where's my room?"

Excited to see them, Peanut jumped around Lynn's feet while Alley Cat settled comfortably in a chair in the living room.

Anya replied, "There are ten bedrooms. Would you like to see yours?"

"Yes!" Lynn exclaimed excitedly.

"Where's the bathroom?" Cindy asked.

"I have to go pee-pee too!" Lynn announced.

"There's a bathroom near my study if you need to go right away," Anya replied. "Otherwise, there's one between your two bedrooms. Cora can show you to your rooms. Maya, Shelley, let's meet in the study for a quick meeting before we start work."

"Cora is pretty," Lynn remarked as she followed the android up the marble staircase. Cindy trailed behind, admiring the elegant steps.

An hour later, the three women joined Max and Lance in the study.

Anya said, "Okay, we'll leave in ten minutes for the lab, and we should be back in a couple of hours. It's just a brief team meeting and updates. Shelley, I think we'll need an extra vehicle for all of us. Can you arrange for your car to arrive here by tomorrow?"

"Sure, I'll take care of it," Shelley tapped on her watch and summoned her car, Thor, to arrive in the morning.

Chapter 23

# Shattered Bonds

"Some wounds never truly heal, and bleed again at the slightest touch." - *J.R.R. Tolkien.*

Anya's voice was heavy as she spoke to Maya and Shelley in her homestead study. "I received news from the police station and also from Sandy's doctor, Dr. Guild. The police provided additional information: Dr. Dee kept a diary that I will review tonight. Dr. Guild informed me that Sandy suffered another epileptic seizure along with a brain aneurysm. They are currently stabilizing her vital signs, managing the seizure with medication, and monitoring her brain function. If her condition worsens, they may need to perform surgical clipping or endovascular coiling to repair the aneurysm. As it stands, she is on a ventilator, and they are managing her intracranial pressure. Unfortunately, Sandy's prognosis does not look good."

Maya and Shelley paused in a shared moment of gravity. Just then, Cindy entered the study and wrapped her arms around Anya's waist. The affection melted Anya's heart.

"Let's go. The lab team is waiting for us," whispered Anya.

"Cindy, we might be late tonight, but Max and Cora will be here with you," Anya assured her. "The meeting should go quickly, and we'll be back for dinner."

Without saying a word, Cindy turned and ran up the stairs and slammed the door to her room.

Lynn entered the office and exclaimed, "Yay! I really like this place. Can Mommy stay with us, too?" Anya asked Max to take Lynn to her room and explain the situation to her again as the women left. Holding Max's hand, Lynn climbed the stairs to her room.

The sudden thud from above snagged Alley Cat's attention. He bolted up the steps and into Lynn's room. Peanut became excited upon seeing the cat and playfully pounced on it. Alley Cat responded by boxing Peanut's nose as a warning, causing the dog to let out a short squeal. Max picked up Peanut to check his nose and assured Lynn that the dog was okay. "Now, Lynn, can we talk about your mommy?" he asked.

***

As Anya, Maya, and Shelley entered the Viral Genesis Laboratory in Corn Hill, New York, they were warmly greeted by Dr. Banker, the supervising scientist at Anya's lab facility, along with four other scientists. The group exchanged greetings and expressed their condolences for the losses everyone had experienced.

Later, Maya and Shelley introduced Lance to the team while Dr. Banker followed Anya into her office to consolidate their work. Anya noticed Dr. Banker limping on one leg.

"What happened to your leg?"

Dr. Banker, who was 38 years old and had gray curls at the temples of her dark brown hair, replied: "It's nothing. I tripped in the dark while getting water, silly me."

"I hope you recover quickly. Does it hurt?"

Dr. Banker, brushing a lock of hair away from her expertly drawn eyebrows, replied, "No, not much. I'm a quick healer. I'll be okay."

Anya glanced at the papers stacked on her desk, "Are these the current data?"

"Yes, these are the reports and results for insemination and incubation."

Anya put her lab coat on. Dr. Banker pulled a chair over to Anya's desk, and the two women began reviewing the research analysis.

Meanwhile, in another lab, Maya and Shelley were demonstrating Lance's advanced enhancements for the team of scientists.

"Lance can lift and push over 1,000 kilograms (2,200 pounds) without damaging the outer layer of his skin," Maya explained.

Dr. Cone, the lab's resident doctor, had cropped blonde hair and a perpetually calm, professional expression. She touched Lance's arm and asked, "What will happen if Lance gets cut?"

Dr. Cone's touch prompted Lance to respond, "Hello, can I help you?"

"Stand down, big boy," Shelley joked with a grin directed at Lance. The others laughed.

Maya picked up a surgical knife and sliced Lance's forearm before stepping back. Lance's eyes immediately dropped to examine the wound. They blinked twice, and his optic lens changed to an amethyst-purple glow, projecting a translucent beam of lilac and deep purple. Focusing on the cut, the wound vanished completely within three seconds. The team exclaimed, "Wow! Amazing!"

"We can show you more later. Shelley and I need to finalize Lance's reproductive compartment in the other room," Maya asked, "Did the specimens arrive?"

Winona Binesi, a focused young woman in her early twenties with long black hair pulled back neatly and a genuinely open, trusting face, replied, "Yes. I'll take you there."

Winona led Maya and Shelley to the adjacent room where the lab housed all the necessary tools: an automated liquid-handling system, robotic arms, sensors, controllers, computers, fabrication tools, power supplies, various actuators, and specialized software.

"Here it is," Winona said, pointing to three cryo storage units on the lab bench.

"Perfect! Thank you," Maya replied.

***

Anya and Dr. Banker reviewed files in Anya's office. Anya remarked, "This is fantastic! Could you show me the blood type charts for each individual?" Dr. Banker began to explain the chart when Anya unexpectedly received a phone call.

"I'm sorry, but I need to take this; it's about Mrs. Evans," Anya said.

"Yes, of course, I'll step outside."

"Hello, Dr. Guild—Yes—Yes, I'll be there. Thank you for calling," Anya said.

When she opened the office door, she saw Dr. Banker waiting nearby. Anya announced, "I have to go, but I will try to return to review the list."

"Fly safely."

Anya entered the next room, interrupting Maya and Shelley as they demonstrated Lance's features. "Dr. Guild called. I'm heading to the hospital," she said. Anya glanced at the wall clock and added, "I should be back this evening before dinner."

Maya asked, "Is it about Sandy?"

"Yes, Dr. Guild said her brain waves have stopped. There's nothing more we can do for her."

Shelley pulled a tissue from beneath her coat sleeve and wiped her eyes. Maya's eyes welled up with tears. She stepped forward to face Anya and said, "I'm so sorry." She added, "Aunt Anya, is there anything I can do?"

Anya shook her head. "No, if I'm late, please have Thor take the three of you back home."

***

Anya flew back to Florida and stood by Mrs. Evan's side, holding her hand. Dr. Guild and an android nurse entered the room.

Anya positioned herself near the bed, watching as the android turned off the life support. Witnessing the woman she loved as a mother slip away was horrifying. Pressing her lips together, she turned her gaze away, tears streaming down her face.

Dr. Guild approached Anya, wrapped her arms around her, and said, "I'm so sorry for your loss. Take your time." She left the room, followed by the android nurse.

Anya approached the lifeless body and took Sandy's hand in hers, whispering, "I will miss you, my dear friend."

Anya's watch instantly lit up; a message from Max, informing her that he had received and downloaded a police report updating information about Dr. Dee.

Anya tapped her watch with a reply, "Wait until I return to the house." She bent over and kissed Sandy's cheek, saying, "I hope you find peace with Barney in the heavens above. Goodbye."

Chapter 24

# For the Love of Man

"Hope deferred makes the heart sick, but a desire fulfilled is a tree of life." - *Proverbs.*

As Anya was leaving the hospital, Max hailed her again.

"Yes, Max, what is it?" she asked.

"Miss Lynn is crying and asking for her mother. She mentioned that she left her doll back in Florida. What should I do?"

"I'm in Florida right now. Ask Lynn to describe the doll. I will stop by her house and pick it up."

"Understood," Max said.

Meanwhile, at the Blaney's house in Florida, Anya searched Lynn's bedroom and found several dolls that matched the description. She gathered them up and flew back to the mansion in Rochester, New York.

Upon entering the house, she noticed the girls in the study with Max, who was teaching them a foreign language. Cindy ran up to her and said in French, "I would like cake." Anya smiled and replied in French, "I would like cake, too."

Max linked with Kit and asked the unit to make a cake. Lynn struggled to understand French and asked, "What did you say?"

Cindy translated the French for Lynn. Afterward, Anya added, "I guess we are having cake soon."

"My dolls." Lynn happily shouted as she retrieved her dolls from Anya's arms. "Sara," Lynn exclaimed, hugging one doll tightly and dropping the others on the floor. Lynn whined to Anya, "Do I have to learn French?"

Instead of answering Lynn, Anya asked Cindy, "How many languages do you know?"

Cindy paused for a moment before replying, "I learned four languages. Do sign language and English count?"

"Of course," Anya responded.

"Then I know six languages. Would you like me to tell you what they are?"

"Sure."

"I know German, Italian, Chinese, Spanish, English, and sign language. Max said he is going to teach us Russian next month."

Lynn became excited. Can I tell you how many languages I learned, Aunt Anya?"

"I would love to hear how many you know, Lynn. Yes, please tell me."

Lynn began to count on her fingers while reciting, "I know… one, two, three. I know three: English, Spanish, and sing language."

Anya asked, "You mean sign language?"

Lynn giggled. "Yes, sign language."

When Cindy chuckled, Lynn shouted, "Don't laugh at me, Cindy!"

"Sing language…ha ha." Cindy laughed louder.

"Aunt Anya, Cindy is laughing at me!"

"Girls, be nice. Good for you, Lynn; it takes time. When you reach Cindy's age, you'll be familiar with most of those languages. I must return to work now. Max, please continue with their lessons."

"Do you have to go now, Aunt Anya?" asked Lynn.

"I won't be gone long; the day is almost over. I'll see you soon."

"Open your math book to chapter seven," Max said.

***

Anya quickly made her way to Carl-23 and flew back to her lab office in New York, resuming work with Dr.

Banker. They reviewed the team reports, and Anya suggested, "Let's bring Winona Binesi into the office."

Dr. Banker tapped on her watch, and Winona entered Anya's office.

Anya said, "Hello, Winona. Please take a seat. I have reviewed your medical report. Five months ago, you were the first person and our youngest staff member to receive the new antivirus serum through our lottery. I also see that you have an AB-negative blood type. Have you experienced any complications?"

Winona smiled. "I feel great so far. Please call me Thunderbird. It has been my nickname since I was a baby, and everyone here calls me that."

"Thunderbird it is. It's a pleasure to meet you. I'm glad we found a suitable sperm bank that offers your lineage to help continue your Native American heritage. Have you had a chance to read the contract and review the detailed pregnancy instruction manual?"

"Yes."

Anya sifted through Thunderbird's documents, "Perfect! I see you understand the complication of a miscarriage could arise. How do you feel about that?"

"I am willing to try again and again until we successfully restore the male population. I've always wanted a large family."

Anya checked Thunderbird's doctor's visit log and said, "Your last exam was about three weeks ago. I want you to see Dr. Cone again in two days for another examination. Please arrange a time with her."

Thunderbird smiled, revealing her beautiful, pearly white teeth, and said, "I will. Thank you, Dr. Peters."

Please call me Anya. I'll speak with you again later. In the meantime, please ask Dr. Sheen to come into the office."

"Thank you, Anya. I will let her know."

After Thunderbird left the office, Anya remarked to Dr. Banker, "I see in these files that they all seem to be doing well in their pregnancies so far."

"Yes, so far," and she pointed out the different serums that each scientist and staff member received in their files. She added, "This experience has challenged these scientists. They sometimes fear losing their babies, but they remain determined not to give up for the love of man. Dr. Sheen previously had an early miscarriage. She requested to try again after two weeks, but Dr. Cone advised her to wait a month. Now, Dr. Sheen is fifteen weeks pregnant and appears to be doing well."

At that moment, Thunderbird burst into the office and exclaimed, "Dr. Mattson is bleeding; they are taking her into our medical lab."

Anya asked, "Is Dr. Cone with her?"

"Yes," Thunderbird replied.

Anya rushed out of the office, followed closely by Dr. Banker. Meanwhile, Dr. Mattson, a young-looking thirty-year-old woman with a subtle cleft palate, was wheeled onto a gurney, blood dripping onto the floor. The scientists moved into action. Dr. Banker and Anya stepped back to observe as Dr. Cone issued orders to rescue the 4-month-old male fetus. While watching the doctor's work, Anya noticed a two-inch cut on the inside of Dr. Cone's left palm when the doctor removed her gloves. Dr. Cone announced loudly, "The baby's heartbeat is strong, and the cervix is closed."

Dr. Banker asked Anya if she would like to visit the other lab rooms while they worked on Dr. Mattson. Anya agreed, and they entered the adjoining lab. Anya's eyes scanned the room filled with incubators. She approached one and saw a deceased male newborn who had tragically succumbed to the Y-Plague. The scientists used these incubated bodies to research a cure. Saddened by the sight, Anya lowered her head and began to weep softly.

Chapter 25

# The Missing Child

"What we see depends mainly on what we look for." - *John Lubbock*.

Dr. Banker approached Anya and said, "I'm sorry; I know this is very difficult to witness. Should we continue to the other rooms?" Anya glanced at the lifeless infant one more time and let out a sorrowful sigh. "Yes, please."

As they left the room, Thunderbird met them and said, "Dr. Mattson requested that we contact Senator Stever."

"Okay, give her a call." Dr. Banker responded.

"Alright," Thunderbird nodded before leaving.

Anya asked, "Is that Dr. Mattson's partner? I didn't know Alex Stever was a senator."

"Yes." Dr. Banker opened the door to the next room, revealing more items. "Here are some of the antiviral vaccines we've used so far, including those that some of our scientists have administered during their pregnancies." The scientist lifted a tube and added, "This is the serum vial given to Dr. Mattson."

They walked over to the refrigerated section. Dr. Banker stated, "This contains the vaccine batches from our latest trials developed over the past two days. These antiviral vaccines, we hope, will counteract the carriers of the Y virus. We also have a cold box in another room for Maya and Shelley."

Turning to Anya, Dr. Banker asked, "Has any female been found who is not a carrier?"

"I checked this morning with laboratories around the world and contacted the AI hub center; none of them have found a single uninfected female."

Dr. Banker opened a door along the hallway and stepped into another room. Anya discovered all her advanced high-tech equipment in a sterile environment, complete with specialized incubators for early-stage embryonic development. However, a deep sense of mourning washed over her as she noticed the unsuccessful, lifeless embryos and fetuses from various trimesters still present in some of the cloning chambers.

"I'm sorry you had to see this, Dr. Peters. The LabAIs haven't cleared this room yet. I'll take care of that."

A person appeared at the door and asked, "Where can I find Dr. Kelly Mattson?"

Dr. Banker replied, "Hello, Senator Stever. You already know Dr. Peters."

Anya reached out her hand. "Hello, Alex ... Kelly is down the hall on the right, in the medical room. Would you like me to take you there?"

Senator Stever, a powerful woman in her early forties with sharp, intelligent eyes, short, styled red hair, and an impeccably tailored suit, shook Anya's hand. "I'm so glad to see you again. Yes, please do, Anya."

The three women returned to the medical room where Dr. Mattson was resting, and the senator hurried to her side, asking, "Oh, honey, are you okay?" The senator leaned over and kissed Dr. Mattson on the forehead.

With tears in her eyes, she nodded in response.

Dr. Cone explained, "Dr. Mattson is a little disoriented. We administered a relaxant, and we've successfully stopped the bleeding. I want her to stay in bed here overnight, and I will remain here with her."

The senator let out a deep sigh and added, "Good, I'll stay here too."

Dr. Cone stated, "Dr. Mattson is going to be out of it through the night. Senator, she won't even notice that you're here."

Anya assured the senator that Dr. Cone would take good care of her. "Alex, if you'd like, you can have dinner with me and spend the night at my place."

The senator looked at Kelly with loving, concerned eyes before turning to Anya and saying, "I would like that, thank you."

***

Anya left the clinic room for her office and received a call from Max. The watch displayed an image of Max wearing one of her father's swimming shorts, goggles over his eyes, and fins on his feet.

"You're not in the water, are you?"

"No."

"Then why are you wearing those items?"

"Lynn told me I should wear these since we're going to the swimming pool." Anya giggled at the sight of Max in pink flamingo swimming trunks.

"Alright, Max, what's going on?"

Max responded, "Lynn isn't here."

"Can you explain, Max?"

"Lynn finished helping me get dressed by the pool and informed me she was going to the kitchen to have Kit make us lemonade," he explained.

"Where is Cora?"

Max pulled off his goggles. "She took Billy to the market for grocery shopping."

"Where is Cindy?"

Max turned his head and saw Cindy splashing about. "She is swimming in the pool."

"Where is Lynn's watch?"

Max responded, "Sensors indicate there has been no movement in the kitchen for the past five minutes. I went to the kitchen and found Lynn's watch on the counter."

"What were Lynn's last words?"

Max played a recording of Lynn's voice saying, "Can we go to my house? Mommy is waiting for me there."

"Max, how did you respond to her?"

Max played the recorded reply he had given to Lynn: "You can ask Anya when she returns from work."

The recording revealed that Lynn had yelled: "No, I want to ask her now!"

There was a brief pause in the recording before Lynn's voice continued, "Can I go to the kitchen and get lemonade for Cindy and me?"

Max responded, "Yes," and a timestamp played the recorded conversation.

Anya glanced at the time and said, "Max, please watch over Cindy and go ahead with your plans for the day. Let me know when Lynn returns. I'm going to look for her."

"Understood."

After the call, Anya approached Dr. Banker, saying, "Sharon, I have a family emergency and need to leave now. I'll get back to you soon." She walked over to Senator Stever, who was gently caressing Dr. Mattson's hair.

"Senator Stever?"

"Please call me Alex; we've been friends for a long time, so there's no need for formality."

"Alex, I need to leave now. Feel free to come over and have dinner with us. You still remember where I live?" Anya asked.

"If you haven't moved, I remember exactly where."

Anya and the senator embraced, and Anya gently stroked Dr. Mattson's hair, saying, "Hang in there, kid. I'll see you later."

Dr. Mattson, dazed from the medication, smiled at Anya and tried to express her gratitude. However, her words came out discombobulated, and she ended up saying, "Drank shoe."

Giggles echoed in the room as Anya called for her car to come pick her up outside.

Realizing she hadn't informed Maya about her plans. Anya entered the lab where Maya and Shelley were conducting their experiment. Maya was holding open the panel that covered Lance's pelvic and groin area, while Shelley had the semen collection container in her hand.

"Sorry to interrupt, but I need to search for Lynn," Anya said. Both Maya and Shelley gasped.

"Where's Lynn?" Maya asked.

"Max reported her missing. I don't know where she is, but I'm going to look for her. By the way, Senator Alex Stever is joining us for dinner."

Shelley's eyes widened as she exclaimed, "Is that 'the' Alex Stever? Wow! Can I join you for dinner?"

"Yes, and yes. But I have to go, bye." Anya dashed out of the building.

Chapter 26

# Wander and Wait

"Truth, like gold, is to be obtained not by its growth, but by washing away all that is not gold." - *Leo Tolstoy.*

Anya ascended into the sky while Carl-23 reduced its speed. She searched her neighborhood, reasoning the child couldn't have wandered too far. Carl-23 hovered silently 500 feet above the ground. Anya commanded the car to magnify the screen by 50% and scan the outdoor surroundings for any signs of the child.

Carl-23 announced, "None found."

Anya commanded the vehicle, "Fly over the next street and continue scanning."

After ten minutes, Carl-23 spotted two children playing three streets away from her mansion. Anya zoomed in with her device and saw Lynn and another girl playing on the sidewalk.

Carl-23 landed, and Anya approached the girls.

"Is this your new friend?" she asked Lynn.

Lynn jumped with excitement, "Aunt Anya, you're here! Yes, this is my friend ..." Lynn realized they hadn't introduced themselves yet.

"I'm Elsie," the five-year-old chimed in, her bright eyes dancing beneath dark braids tied with colorful ribbons.

"I'm Lynn."

Anya looked around searching for Elsie's android. It seemed unusual to find a child without their android guardian. The door to Elsie's mansion opened, and an android carrying a fresh batch of chocolate chip cookies approached them. As he lowered the tray, he said, "Hello, I'm Clay. Would you like a cookie?"

Elsie eagerly grabbed one and offered, "You can have some too."

Lynn looked up at Anya, seeking approval. "Can I have a cookie, please?" she asked.

"You can have one, too," Elsie said to Anya.

With cookies in hand, Anya added, "Miss Lynn, we should head back to the house; your sister and Max are worried about you."

"Okay," Lynn said with a smile, "Can I see Elsie again?"

"Yes, but you should ask Max to bring you and your sister next time so that Elsie can meet Cindy."

"Okay." Lynn skips along the sidewalk toward Carl-23.

Elsie stood by Clay, waving goodbye.

The weather shifted from sunny to threatening thunderstorms. Anya could not fly Carl-23. Lightning bolts streaked across the sky. Instead, they drove home.

"Miss Lynn, we were all worried about you," Anya said firmly. "Why did you take off your watch and leave the house?"

Lynn bit into her piece of cookie and replied, "I need to find my way home to the watch."

Anya picked the crumbs off Lynn's bathing suit. "And how do you find your way home without your watch?"

Lynn shrugged, "I don't know."

"Why did you leave the house, Lynn?"

"Max told me that I have to ask you if I can go home and see Mommy."

"You could have asked Max to call me. Lynn, do you still want to go home?"

Lynn took another nibble and looked up at Anya, "No, Mommy is gone now."

Anya guided Lynn back inside the mansion. As they walked through the grand entrance, Cindy ran to her sister, her face red with worry. She cried out in a trembling voice, "Lynn, where did you go?"

Lynn shrugged, displaying a carefree attitude that heightened Cindy's concern.

Anya stepped inside and said, "Lynn made a new friend named Elsie, and she's not going to leave the house by herself anymore, right, Lynn?"

Lynn nodded, and Anya sent the girls with Max into the study for their afternoon lessons.

***

The thunderstorm continued, making flying too risky. Carl-23 drove Anya back to her lab in Corn Hill, New York. She made a beeline for Dr. Mattson's clinical room, where the scientist rested with a faint smile. The senator stood at her side. Dr. Mattson, a brilliant 27-year-old science researcher who was four months pregnant, faced a heartbreaking reality: the possibility of losing her unborn son due to the experiments intended to bring back the male species.

After visiting Dr. Mattson, Anya returned to her office and began checking on the progress of each pregnant member of the science staff. Dr. Sheen entered Anya's office.

Dr. Sheen, who was usually composed, had fine brown hair, typically pulled back into a strict bun. However, she appeared fatigued.

Noticing Dr. Sheen's pale complexion, Anya said, "I see that you are 23 weeks into your pregnancy...Have you felt the baby move?"

"Yes, I'm feeling subtle flutters, almost like butterflies under my skin."

Anya reviewed Dr. Sheen's files and spoke with concern in her voice, "You've been working too many hours, and it's starting to show. You look pale, dear. I'll schedule an appointment for you with Dr. Cone tomorrow and ask Dr. Banker to give you some time off to rest, okay?"

"I could use a couple of days to recuperate. I haven't slept much. May I return in two days?"

"Absolutely. If you need more time to rest, just let us know. Otherwise, we'll see you soon."

"I will. Thank you, Dr. Peters."

But, before Dr. Sheen left the office, Anya noticed a dark, rusty spot near Dr. Sheen's sleeve and asked: "Margaret, is that blood on your lab coat?"

Dr. Sheen laughed, "Oh, I spilled ketchup on it during lunch a few days ago. I thought I wiped it all off, but it dried and stained immediately. These white coats show everything."

After Dr. Sheen left, Dr. Ibarra walked in. She was a meticulous researcher with dark brown skin and a shoulder-length haircut, who often wore conservative brown-framed glasses. She removed her glasses and placed them in the pocket of her lab coat. "I'm still experiencing morning sickness."

"I'm sorry that you're experiencing that. Has Dr. Cone prescribed anything for you?"

Dr. Ibarra paced in Anya's office, "Not yet, I need to eat small, frequent, bland meals. Dr. Cone also told me to stay hydrated and take ginger. It helped a little, but …" Immediately, Dr. Ibarra felt a gag reflex coming on. She quickly grabbed a tissue from her pocket, covered her mouth, looked at Anya with her concerned pale brown eyes, and dashed out of the office.

Anya called out, "See Dr. Cone in the morning!"

As Dr. Ibarra hurried to the bathroom, she passed Dr. Cone in the hallway. The doctor called out to her, "I want to see you tomorrow!"

When Dr. Cone entered Anya's office, she removed her cap, revealing her thick, red copper curls. "What a day," she exclaimed.

Anya replied, "I understand how you feel. It's not over yet." She noticed the cut on Dr. Cone's hand again and asked, "That cut looks nasty. How did it happen?"

Dr. Cone looked embarrassed. "Have you ever placed a glass in a full, soapy sink and forgotten it was there?" Dr. Cone shook her head, "Well, I did that while moving things around, I accidentally broke the glass while reaching into the dishpan. Boy, did it hurt. It took a while for the bleeding to stop."

"Wow! How long ago did that happen?"

Dr. Cone shrugged. "I think it was less than a week ago … maybe longer."

"Good thing you didn't need stitches."

"Yeah, I'm lucky it wasn't a deep cut."

"Okay," Anya said, glancing at the files. "Please reexamine everyone tomorrow and fit them into your schedule. I want an update on their conditions."

"No problem," Dr. Cone replied, "I can do that. Dr. Mattson is managing, but there's not much more I can do for her. We'll keep her off her feet for a couple of days, and I'll assign her some research papers to keep her occupied."

Anya asked, "How are you doing?"

"I'm experiencing some swelling and discomfort in my feet that's normal for this trimester … Are you sure you want to proceed with this, Anya?"

Anya met the doctor's gaze. "Mona, we've already made our decision. I can't back out; I'm part of the lottery. In ten days, I'll reach my prime ovulation."

Dr. Cone placed her cap on her head, tucking her hair neatly underneath it. "I want to examine you with this new serum that's coming up here from your Florida lab.

"Of course. Have you seen Dr. Banker?"

"She and Thunderbird are preparing a room for the senator to sleep here tonight."

"Where is the senator?"

"She's still with Dr. Mattson." When her watch alerted her that it was time to see Dr. Ibarra, Dr. Cone apologized and left Anya's office.

Anya called out, "Thank you. I'll see you tomorrow after you finish all your exams with the others."

Chapter 27

# A Glimmer of New Order

"The old order changeth, yielding place
to new." - *Alfred, Lord Tennyson.*

Dr. Banker limped into Anya's office and said, "Everyone is back at their benches working except for Dr. Mattson and Dr. Sheen. Dr. Cone will stay in the next room tonight if Dr. Mattson needs her. I'll be here until everyone leaves."

"Got it. Let's continue our rounds in the building." As they walked through the hallway, they encountered Senator Stever. Dr. Banker excused herself, leaving Anya and the senator to talk.

The senator said, "I'm looking forward to having dinner with you, but I won't be staying the night. I'll be with Kelly. Is that alright with you?"

"Yes, of course. Feel free to come by anytime after 5 p.m. I'm looking forward to your visit."

The senator responded, "Me too. I'm heading out to grab a few things from my house to bring back to Kelly. I'll see you later, and thank you."

By the end of the day, Anya and Dr. Banker began closing down the labs. The LabAIs' soft humming hardly filled the air, but their twinkling processors illuminated the lab rooms like Christmas lights.

Anya complimented the scientist, saying, "Those are lovely pearl earrings you're wearing."

"Thank you," replied Dr. Banker.

Anya continued, "Blue? I didn't know pearls could be such a deep blue. It's such a beautiful color."

"They are natural blue pearls, which are considered rare and more valuable."

"Beautiful … Did the senator receive a temporary passcode to reenter after hours?"

"Yes…By the way, what are your plans for your Florida lab? Have you heard anything from the police station about Dr. Dee's death?"

"I did receive a report, but I haven't read it yet. I plan to go over it this evening."

"I'll see you tomorrow," Dr. Banker called out to Anya. As Dr. Banker felt the rain sprinkle on her head, she quickly limped to her car.

***

Back at the mansion, Senator Alex Stever arrived at Anya's home, and the conversation remained light with most attention focused on Cindy and Lynn. Just as Max was about to take the girls away, curious Lynn asked, "Hey, lady, are you going to play games with us in the playroom?"

The senator smiled. "I'll try, but I can't stay too long tonight. May I take a rain check?"

Lynn ran to the front door and, after opening it, shouted: "It's not raining anymore; it's just sprinkling outside."

Seated at the table, Cindy called, "No, Lynn, don't go to the door; you should look out the window." Everyone giggled with delight, and Anya called out, "Lynn, come here, honey."

Lynn closed the door and ran back, saying, "It's sprinkling outside. Are you going to play with us, lady?"

Anya explained, "Senator Stever meant that we can do this later or at another time."

"Then why did she tell me to check the rain?" Lynn asked. Meanwhile, Cindy got up from her seat, and Cora picked up her plate.

"Lynn, Max will explain it to you. Max, please take the girls to the playroom and clarify the phrase 'raincheck' for them." Anya said.

"Understood," replied Max as he walked across the hall to the bathroom where the girls could wash their hands and brush their teeth after dinner. Afterward, they headed to the study for an explanation and some games.

"Alex, may Shelley and I ask you some questions?" Maya asked.

"Of course."

Everyone left their seats and moved into the guest living room while Cora cleared the dishes. Alex, a 42-year-old, intelligent, and poised woman, sat quietly in a chair near the fireplace, emanating a powerful presence with her calm demeanor.

Anya was the first to speak. She asked Alex, "How did you meet Kelly?"

The senator explained that she and Dr. Mattson met through their husbands, who were long-time friends. "Tragically, both of our husbands passed away before the Y-Plague. Brad, Kelly's husband, was killed in a hunting accident, and my husband, Eric, died eight months later from an aneurysm. After experiencing our losses, we formed a strong bond and eventually became companions." The senator concluded by saying, "We've been together for three years now."

Shelley said, "I'm sorry, everyone, but I have to leave soon to visit my mother and stay with her overnight." She turned to the senator and asked, "May I ask you a question before I go?"

"Sure."

"How are things politically now that we no longer have men in leadership positions?"

The senator smiled and replied, "Initially, it was challenging, but things are running smoothly now. However, some areas still require improvement, particularly in collaborative leadership. We place a strong emphasis on community, education, and child-rearing, with a special focus on emotional intelligence, critical thinking, and empathy."

The senator lifted her cup of hot chocolate, took a sip, and continued, "Additionally, we concentrate on AI-powered justice and security systems that analyze data to predict and prevent crime. Women are taking leadership roles in restorative justice programs, prioritizing rehabilitation and community healing. With women in positions of power, we emphasize social welfare and conflict resolution. This shift has resulted in a decrease in violent crime, particularly in cases of domestic violence, rape, and murder."

The senator stood up from her seat, walked over to the window, and glanced outside. "We actively participate in peacebuilding and conflict resolution processes to achieve more sustainable peace agreements, which have proven effective. Now that wars are over, thank God, we reprogrammed the AI combatants to assist us at home instead of using them for destruction and killing." The senator returned to her chair and sat down.

Maya interjected, "I'm so glad there are no more wars."

The senator continued, "These AI robots now assist everyone with daily tasks. Aged individuals with disabilities receive companionship, medication reminders, and assistance with mobility. Anya, you've seen how diagnostic tools analyze medical images and patient data to detect diseases earlier and more accurately."

"Yes, I have."

The senator checked her watch.

"I'm sorry to interrupt," Shelley said to the group, "but I would love to hear more. I have so many questions about prostitution and drugs, but I need to leave in five minutes. Will we see you again?"

"Yes, I can quickly answer that for you, and I hope to visit again. Generally, prostitution, which is primarily driven by male consumers, has diminished. However, when it comes to drugs, substance use is often linked to social and economic factors. The stress and trauma of living in a world without men have led some individuals to increase their substance use. Moreover, the absence of male-dominated drug distribution networks has disrupted the supply chain."

The senator paused and giggled when she spotted Lynn running down the hall, Peanut chasing after her. She continued, "The government is now addressing the drug addictions that existed both before and after the loss of the male population. Although data collection is underway, these issues still need to be managed. We need to continue focusing on treatment and prevention. Today, artificial intelligence personalizes treatment plans that help monitor and prevent drug-related crimes."

The senator changed the subject, "Shelley, where does your mother live?"

Shelley's mother, Dr. Felicia Brown, had recently developed a revolutionary algae-based BioSkin that provides waterproof protection and enhances solar energy efficiency. This BioSkin offers a lifelike appearance with customizable anatomical features. Additionally, the nanotechnology-based skin has a human-like texture and maintains a constant temperature. The android, Lance, Dr. Brown's first experiment, was given to Shelley and Maya for testing and reproduction.

"My mother is in Michigan." Shelley looked over at Anya and Maya, "I'll see you tomorrow, goodnight," she said.

The senator stood up, "I should get back to Kelly. Thank you for dinner. I'll see you tomorrow, Anya."

"Yes, and if you have any problems getting into the building, just contact me."

"Will do."

Maya headed to the study to focus on Lance while the kids settled into their bedrooms for the night. After visiting each child, hugging them, and saying goodnight,

Anya went to her room. She started reading the reports on Dr. Dee by flipping through the digital documents on her watch. Dr. Dee, the woman who had saved her life from the lab fire, was now shrouded in mystery. Anya's eyes widened, and she gasped as she read: *'An investigation is underway to solve a homicide, arson, and forgery, with the involvement of an accomplice.*

Chapter 28

# The Forger's Shadow

"The truth is rarely pure and never simple." - *Oscar Wilde.*

Anya's sleep was a restless sea of fragmented thoughts, her mind swirling with unanswered questions. However, the morning brought Cindy's amusing stories and Lynn's joyful laughter, helping lift Anya's worries.

After breakfast, Anya briefed Maya on her itinerary for the day, and they headed to the lab. Once there, Maya joined Shelley to fine-tune Lance, preparing the android for its upcoming assignment. If they succeeded, they would be able to manufacture Lance models in large quantities within a month. Anya also visited Dr. Mattson in the lab to check on her condition.

Dr. Cone informed Anya, "She is restless but recovering well. The bleeding has stopped, and I'm monitoring her closely. If you're looking for the senator, she just left, but she mentioned she would return as soon as Dr. Mattson needs her."

"Thank you."

"By the way, will you be around for your exam?" Dr. Cone asked.

"I will be out for most of the day, and I'm not sure how long it will take. May I meet you at the end of the day for an update on everyone's pregnancy status?"

"Yes."

***

Anya directed Carl-23 to fly her to the police station in Florida to seek answers. However, the TrackAI refused to provide any details without clearance from Officer Stanley, who remained tight-lipped about the ongoing investigation. Frustrated, Anya returned to Dr. Dee's house to conduct her own investigation and get a closer look at the crime scene.

At Dr. Dee's house, the front door was locked, but the back door opened easily. Inside, the bathroom presented a chilling scene: dried blood stained the empty tub. The bedroom provided little comfort as she entered, searching for clues that might explain Dr. Dee's death and the note on the credenza. She opened the closet door, still unsure of what she was looking for, but her instincts told her that something felt off about the closet. Since she couldn't put her finger on it, she decided to go into the kitchen. She noticed two empty teacups sitting near the sink, but nothing else appeared unusual.

Anya returned to the bedroom and stood in the doorway, contemplating the furniture. She noticed two nightstands, one on each side of the bed. Opening a drawer to search for clues, she was startled by a voice.

"Are you looking for something?"

Anya turned quickly to see Officer Stanley standing by the bedroom door, accompanied by a TrackAI.

"You surprised me … I'm just searching for answers since you won't help me."

"It's an open case," Officer Stanley replied. "I still need to speak with all of your scientists first. Don't worry, I'll update you once we have more information."

Anya turned to leave, but Officer Stanley called her back. "One more thing," the officer said, projecting an image on her watch. "Do you recognize this handwriting?"

"Yes, it's Dr. Dee's."

"Take another look," Officer Stanley urged, zooming in on the script. "It's a forgery."

"What? How can you tell?"

Officer Stanley hesitated before responding. "Dr. Dee kept a diary hidden between the mattress and the box spring. Our crime lab found no match between the diary and the letter addressed to you in terms of handwriting. While there were some similarities, it wasn't an exact match. Someone attempted to copy her handwriting but couldn't replicate the strokes and curves correctly." Officer Stanley ended the projection on her watch. "I don't think the killer knew the scientist had a diary. The diary implicates a lover named Peaches."

Anya pressed, "What about the fingerprints on the tea setting?"

Officer Stanley interrupted her, "That's all I'll say."

With her mind racing, Anya decided to stop by her house in Florida to pick up fresh clothes rather than buy anything new. However, a news reporting android unit was waiting, ready to broadcast to the media if it detected Anya near her home. Fortunately, her projects and the location of her father's house remained top secret from the public.

Anya made one last stop at the charred remains of her Florida lab. As she walked around, she was uncertain about what she was searching for. She recalled seeing parts of the women's bodies behind the benches lying on the floor. The blackened walls and the oppressive silence filled her with unease.

"What are you doing here?" Dr. Croft's voice called out.

"I'm looking for clues … What are you doing here?"

"I came to collect anything that the fire hadn't damaged and take it to the new location. Are you planning to visit the new lab?"

"Not today. I'll be in touch soon."

Anya returned to her laboratory in New York and sought assistance from Senator Alex Stever, successfully gaining access to Dr. Dee's police report.

***

Anya was about to read the report in her office when she received a call from Dr. Cone. "Dr. Mattson went into labor, and unfortunately, her baby boy was born prematurely and passed away an hour ago. I administered a tranquilizer to help her sleep," Dr. Cone explained.

"I'm on my way to see Dr. Mattson now."

When Anya got to Dr. Mattson's room, the senator was holding her hand. Anya approached the senator and hugged her, softly saying, "I'm so sorry for your loss."

"Thank you. Kelly is strong; we'll get through this."

"I want to thank you for helping me get the report. I really appreciate it."

The senator wiped the tears from her face and replied gently, "You're welcome. I sent my Chief of Staff, Maggie Henderson, who knew exactly which buttons to press. Henderson informed the Chief of Police that this had national security implications related to your work. They released the information under the guise of agency cooperation to avoid an official hearing. You have the raw data, but it didn't come easy. I hope you find out who did this. If you need anything else, just let me know."

Dr. Cone entered the room and approached Dr. Mattson's bed. She faced Anya and said, "I'm here to check on her. Anya, I'll see you after."

Anya returned to her office and began to read the police files. Moments later, Dr. Cone peeked in and asked, "Is this a good time for me to update you on everyone's reports?"

Anya turned off her projected watch and took the reports from Dr. Cone.

"I can begin examining you at 4 o'clock. Will you be ready, Anya?"

"Yes, 4 p.m. works for me."

Anya opened Dr. Sheen's file, which contained the medical records of a 28-year-old woman in her second trimester. The chart included details on all vaccination series and test results received before and after conception, along with updates from prenatal check-ups. Once she finished reviewing Dr. Sheen's record, Anya set the file aside and picked up Dr. Ibarra's file to read.

She heard a knock on her door. Dr. Banker peeked inside and said, "Dr. Cone is ready to see you."

Anya glanced at her watch and replied, "Wow! … time has flown by so quickly. Thanks."

Anya underwent a series of tests and immune-boosting treatments in Dr. Cone's clinical room to prepare for the procedure. Robot technicians injected thick vaccines through wide needles, placed dissolving tablets under her tongue, and guided her through controlled inhalations of metallic-tasting vapor. Over the next three days, the inoculations blurred together. Like her staff, she endured fever, aching joints, nausea, and bone-deep fatigue as her body became a battleground for the new formulas.

Ultimately, she fell sick and remained at home for ten days. During this time, she ate less, rested more, and spent hours in bed reading the scientist's diary whenever her head felt clear. She pieced together the fragments of Dr. Dee's hidden love affair. From what she gathered, the woman had only met her lover just over a year ago at a science convention, and the two women instantly hit it off.

In her diary, she expressed her frustration that 'Peaches' never invited her to her home after their initial visit; instead, they spent more time at Dr. Dee's place. Although the scientist kept their relationship a secret, she described their love affair in the diary as passionate and thrilling. Anya experienced a mix of embarrassment as she read about the intimate sexual fantasies shared between the two women. Anya couldn't help but wonder, *Who is Peaches?*

Chapter 29

# Cora's Closet

"The clothes make the man." - *Proverb.*

Anya heard a knock on her bedroom door. She called out, "Come in."

Maya opened the door and asked, "How are you feeling? Do you want Max to bring you some soup? The girls miss you and have been asking about you."

Anya replied, "I feel a bit better, but I still have a headache. I would like to see the girls."

"Okay, I'll have them visit you after they finish their lessons," Maya said. "They want to show you something."

Anya added, "You know, I would enjoy some soup after all. Could Cora make some and deliver it to me? I don't want to interrupt Max while he's tutoring."

Maya promised, "I will do that," and left the room.

Anya got out of bed, brushed her hair, and settled onto her lounger, allowing the sunlight to stream through the window and warm her.

The door opened, and Cora entered with a tray holding a bowl of vegetable soup and crackers.

Cora placed the tray on Anya's lap and said, "I hope you are feeling better."

"Yes, I do feel better, thank you." She looked at the food and added, "You know what I like." Anya realized that her father had programmed Cora to know all of his children's favorite foods.

Cora asked, "Would you like me to close the drapes?"

"No, Cora, please change your dress. I've noticed you've been wearing the same one since we arrived. I know my father loved seeing you in that dress, but he's gone now, and you don't need to wear it every day. I would like you to wear something different each day to set a good example of cleanliness for the girls. And thank you for the soup, Cora. I'll signal you when I finish."

"You are welcome, and yes, I will change my clothing."

The soup and crackers helped calm Anya's stomach. She signaled for Cora to come back. When Cora returned to the room, Anya was flabbergasted and asked, "Cora, what are you wearing?"

"I'm wearing a shirt and pants."

"Are those my father's clothes? Where did you get them?"

"From his closet."

Cora wore baggy men's pants, cinched at the waist with a tight belt. The shirt draped over her shoulders, covering her hands.

"Don't you have any clothes of your own?"

Cora replied, "No."

"What happened to the clothes you had?"

"Your father no longer wanted me to wear any of your mother's items; he donated them to charity."

Cindy and Lynn raced into Anya's room, surprised by Cora's outfit. They began to giggle.

"Why is Cora wearing men's clothes?" Lynn asked.

Cindy jabbed her sister's side and leaned over to whisper in her ear. Lynn and Cindy both made gestures with their hands.

Anya was about to explain when she noticed the girls using sign language. Although Anya only knew a few signs, she recognized what Max had taught them in their lessons.

“Oh, I know this one,” Anya said. “You’re saying, ‘I love you,’ right?”

Lynn jumped up and down, giggling with excitement that Anya understood.

"And you, Cindy, let's see you do it again," Anya continued.

Cindy repeated her sign. Anya responded, "I know you're asking me if I feel better now. Yes, I do, thank you."

Cindy felt proud and walked over to Anya to hug her. Not wanting to be left out, Lynn also jumped into Anya's arms, and the three of them shared a group hug.

Maya peeked into the bedroom and asked, "Anya, are you ready?"

"I will be," Anya replied. "Girls, go downstairs and wait for Maya."

Lynn asked, "Oh, do we have to? We haven't seen you in such a long time."

Cindy added, "Yeah, it's been ten days."

Anya smiled and said, "Then you'll miss out on your adventure."

"Okay, okay," the girls said as they ran out of the room.

"Why is Cora wearing Grandpa's clothes?" Maya asked.

Anya explained the situation and suggested to Maya, Anya explained the situation and suggested to Maya, "Take the girls and Cora shopping. Find outfits for the android."

Maya grinned and said, "Come on, Cora. Go change back into your dress and meet us downstairs."

Cora replied, "Understood," and left the room.

***

"Okay, are you ready?" Maya asked. Anya hesitated for a moment before nodding.

Maya stepped out of the room and soon returned with Lance. She said, "Be gentle with him," and giggled as she added, "Enjoy," before closing the door.

Chapter 30

# The Seed

"Hope is the thing with feathers—That perches in the soul—And sings the tune without the words—And never stops at all." - *Emily Dickinson.*

Anya informed Lance to lock the bedroom door. The android obeyed and stood silent, waiting for further commands. Still grappling with the profound loss of her husband, Anya embarked on a crucial mission: to conceive male offspring to ensure the survival of humanity. Before Andrew's Skypad 5 mission, he had frozen his sperm, a vital resource for their future endeavors. The internal cryogenic compartment in Lance held Andrew's selected XY chromosome specimens, which he had preserved and prepared for implantation. In the future, Lance android models offered women, including her staff, a more intimate and lifelike alternative to the traditional surgical impregnation method that they had once endured. These androids' adaptive biomimetic systems enabled conception through guided biological transfer rather than invasive procedures, reducing trauma and recovery time while preserving genetic integrity.

Anya felt a deep sense of guilt and betrayal, even though she was a widow. Agreeing to the insemination felt like crossing a line she had sworn she would never approach. Lance's presence, his voice, and the careful way he mirrored Andrew's mannerisms blurred the boundary between science and memory. Part of her feared she was not creating new life, but reaching backward, trying to reclaim something already lost. She wondered if this choice honored Andrew's love or quietly replaced it.

Anya ordered the android, "Lance, come over here."

The android obeyed and approached her bedside. Lance asked, "How may I assist you?"

Anya stood before him in silence and disrobed, allowing the soft fabric of her clothing to pool at her feet. Sitting on the edge of the bed, she commanded, "Lance, take off your clothes."

Anya watched as Lance disrobed. Light traced the clean lines of his shoulders and the controlled movement beneath his skin. Muscle shifted smoothly along his arms as he moved, his torso lean and precisely formed, every plane deliberate. His abdomen tightened and released with each breath, engineered strength balanced with human grace, close enough to perfection to feel intentional rather than artificial. She hesitated, unsure about going further. She considered reading the police report instead, but she knew her time with Lance was limited. Everyone would be returning soon after their shopping trip, and she was currently in the middle of her ovulation cycle.

Finally, Anya blurted out, "I'm not sure I want to do this."

Lance placed a hand on her shoulder and gazed into her eyes, saying, "Okay, is there anything I can do to help you feel more comfortable?"

She could barely find the words, and she couldn't believe she felt embarrassed by an android looking at her body, let alone touching her. Taking a deep breath, she said, "Lance, I want you to impregnate me."

Lance replied, "My pleasure. How would you like me to proceed?"

Anya blushed and said, "I would like the missionary position."

Anya lay back on the bed, closed her eyes, and nodded for Lance to continue.

No romance, no passion; only the clinical execution of a necessary act occurred. However, Lance's artificial skin possessed an uncannily lifelike texture. The rhythmic friction of their bodies forged an unusual intimacy. Anya tried to view the experience as natural insemination, but a familiar wave of arousal washed over her, a sensation reminiscent of Andrew, yet distinct from him. Love defined her relationship with Andrew, pure and unadulterated. Lust fueled this moment, and the unexpected surge caught her; she reached her climax. Sensing her response, Lance mirrored her pace. The short sexual encounter ended, and Lance asked, "Would you like me to cuddle with you for a while in bed?"

Anya, on the verge of tears, replied, "No." She grew worried about everyone returning after shopping and asked the android to leave her room. He sat on the edge of the bed and stood up to leave.

As Anya reached for her robe on the floor, she noticed Lance unlocking the bedroom door. Just as he was about to exit, Anya called out, "Lance, please get dressed before you leave."

Lance replied, "Understood." He returned, put on his clothes, and then left.

Anya slid back into bed and thought about Andrew, aware that her memories of him had begun to blur her judgment. She shifted from longing to resolve, reminding herself that nostalgia could not guide the choices ahead. The work demanded clarity, not grief. She slipped her watch back on and checked her schedule for the coming days, grounding herself in routine. An invitation she had forgotten surfaced on the display, a dinner party at Dr.

Banker's home on Saturday at seven. She paused, picturing the room, the conversations, the expectations, and briefly wondered what version of herself would attend. Then she opened the police report, letting duty replace distraction.

***

A few hours later, Anya heard shouting inside the house, followed by the thud of feet racing up the stairs. High, breathless voices called out in unison, "Aunt Anya!" The sound stopped just outside her door. Anya opened it in time to see the girls hesitate, exchange glances, and then burst into laughter before shuffling back down the stairs, their excitement trailing behind them.

Cindy called out, "Close your eyes and don't look, Aunt Anya!"

Lynn shouted at her sister, "I wanted to tell her that!"

Standing at the top of the steps, Anya did what they asked and closed her eyes.

"Okay, you can look now!" Cindy yelled.

Lynn frowned and exclaimed, "I wanted to say that!"

"It's okay, Lynn. I still have my eyes closed; just let me know when to open them." Anya responded.

Lynn, holding Cora's hand, smiled and stuck her tongue out at her sister, saying, "Aunt Anya, you can open your eyes now."

Anya opened her eyes and saw a red-haired woman wearing a sea-blue party dress, standing between the girls. Anya blinked in surprise, realizing it was the android,

Cora, fully dressed in stylish attire, with red-dyed hair and makeup that enhanced her cheekbones.

"Cora, you look stunning," Anya exclaimed, imagining how glamorous her mother would have looked as a redhead.

Lynn added, "Now Cora can get married and have red-haired baby girls."

Cindy laughed and said, "No … Androids don't get married or have babies."

The girls began to argue until Maya entered the house and asked, "Is anyone going to help me?"

From the top floor, Anya watched as the girls rushed to help Maya unload the bags she was carrying. Max strolled into the house after taking Peanut for a walk, while the dog playfully nipped at his ankle.

Anya had hoped for a peaceful night to catch up on her reading, but the girls were full of energy and eager to model Cora's new outfits.

Anya asked, "How many outfits did you get for Cora?"

"Seven, one for each day of the week," Cindy replied.

The girls eagerly took Cora in and out of the study, having her change into different outfits to model for Anya.

After a while, Anya asked, "What number are we on?"

Lynn answered, "Three."

Cindy quickly corrected her, saying, "No … It's her fourth outfit."

Lynn giggled and said, "I forgot."

Anya firmly requested, "Can we see them tomorrow?" and kindly added, "You know it's past your bedtime."

When Anya finally lay down in bed with the police reports, she fell asleep before she could read.

***

The next morning, Dr. Cone examined Anya and updated her on Dr. Mattson's condition.

Anya asked, "Is she here today?"

Dr. Cone replied, "No, but she'll be back on Monday. How about you? Did you see Lance?"

Anya, a bit embarrassed, admitted, "Yes."

Dr. Cone removed the stethoscope and said, "Alright, continue for a week, then I'll recheck you … By the way, are you attending Dr. Banker's dinner party?"

"I plan on it. Are you going?"

"I wouldn't miss it."

"I haven't seen Dr. Banker. Is she here today?" Anya asked.

"No, she took the day off. She's focused on setting up for her party."

At that moment, someone anxiously tapped on Dr. Cone's office door. "Come in." Dr. Cone said.

Dr. Ibarra peeked inside. "Sorry to disturb you, but it's Thunderbird; she passed out in the hallway and has a fever."

Chapter 31

# The Party

"In union there is strength." - *Aesop.*

Two LabAIs activated their sirens, lifting Thunderbird off the floor and transporting her to Dr. Cone's medical examining room, where everyone in the lab had gathered to attend to her.

Dr. Cone examined Thunderbird's eyes and asked, "Thunderbird, can you hear me?" She called out, "Someone, please get me the smelling salts!"

Dr. Sheen quickly retrieved the smelling salts. Dr. Cone held them under Thunderbird's nose. Thunderbird opened her eyes, shook her head, and asked, "Where am I? What happened?"

Dr. Cone replied, "You're in the medical room. Please stay still while I check you over."

Anya directed the others, "Let's run some tests on her."

Maya entered the room and moved to Anya's side to observe as they worked on Thunderbird. They attached an IV solution and checked her blood pressure and body temperature.

Anya's watch signaled an incoming call from Dr. Croft in Florida. Stepping out of the room to take the call, Anya answered, "Hello?"

On the other end of the line, Dr. Croft appeared on the screen, standing in her new lab and holding up a tube. "I have a new serum labeled Y-Cav," she said. "I'll bring it to you at the dinner party. Will you be there?"

"Yes," Anya replied.

"Great! I'm bringing my cousin Julie, who is nine. I hope you'll bring your two girls because I would love for them to meet."

Anya replied, "Yes."

"You sound a bit off. Are you okay?" Dr. Croft asked.

"I'll update you at the dinner party," Anya replied.

"I'm looking forward to meeting Julie. They will be excited to make a new friend."

"Okay, I won't keep you. See you soon. Bye."

Anya returned to the room where they had lowered Thunderbird's temperature, and she was now resting. Dr. Cone asked, "Thunderbird, can your grandma watch over you at home?"

"I don't want to leave; I'll be fine," Thunderbird insisted.

"Let's see how you feel later. I'll check on you a few times today, and if you plan on working, I want you to team up with Dr. Ibarra."

"Okay," Thunderbird replied.

"We'll keep an eye on her," Dr. Cone assured Anya.

By the end of the workday, Thunderbird felt better and decided to head home.

***

On Saturday night, Anya and the girls entered Dr. Banker's party. Lynn, full of youthful energy, spotted other children in the foyer and dashed off with Cora and Cindy following closely behind. Dr. Banker stood near the entrance, warmly welcoming her guests.

"Anya, I'm so glad you could make it. People are mingling in three different rooms. Brutus will ring the bell for dinner soon—Is Maya on her way?"

"Yes, she should be here any minute."

"Wonderful. You haven't been here before, have you?"

"No."

"Before we eat, let me give you a tour once everyone arrives, okay?"

"I look forward to it."

Anya felt a tap on her shoulder. She turned to see Maya, her hair pulled back in a neat braid, wearing a bright dress that shimmered in the light. Her eyes sparkled with excitement.

"I'm here," Maya said, practically bouncing on her heels.

Anya recognized many familiar faces in the room: her teams from New York, Florida, and Texas, along with officials, fellow scientists, and engineers. Mothers cradled their children, androids stood quietly nearby, and everyone seemed caught between duty and curiosity.

Maya spotted Shelley, and the two women slipped away to the family room, joining others their age. The older attendees gravitated toward the study, while the largest group stayed in the living room.

The unintentional age-based segregation gave the women a chance to share the moments only they could understand. Stories of long nights in labs; breakthroughs and failures; losses and triumphs; moments shaped by work, family, and the rare intersections of the two.

After Dr. Croft handed the serum to Anya, she directed Max to place the items in Carl-23.

Thunderbird entered the room and found Anya seated next to her grandmother, Kai. Kai was an older, distinguished woman with long, flowing black hair and gentle eyes.

"Hi, Anya," Thunderbird greeted her before turning to her grandmother. "Did Dr. Banker show you around?"

Kai lifted her head to meet her granddaughter's eyes and replied, "No, dear."

Thunderbird asked Anya, "How about you, Doc?"

"Not yet. How are you feeling, Thunderbird?"

"I don't know why I passed out with a fever, but I feel fine now. Isn't this party exciting? Grandma, they have appetizers in the next room. Doc, would you like to join us?"

Anya's gaze wandered to a coffee table book. She replied, "No, thank you. I'll wait until Dr. Banker shows me around. I'll join you later."

Kai and Thunderbird left the room, and Anya picked up the book, casually flipping through the photographs recording Dr. Banker's various trips around the world. One photo, in particular, stopped her. Dr. Banker was smiling, posed against the turquoise waves of some distant shore, her hair loose and catching the sunlight just so. She wore the same distinctive blue pearl earrings Anya recognized—but now, something new drew her eye: a delicate matching bracelet glinting on her wrist. Anya had never seen it before, and the unexpected detail made her lean closer, studying the photograph as if it might whisper a secret.

Anya was startled when Dr. Banker approached her from behind. "A friend of mine captured this while we were in Italy," she announced.

"Italy, huh? I've always wanted to see Florence," Anya replied.

Dr. Banker chuckled. "Florence is beautiful, but my favorite place is the Amalfi Coast. The coastlines there are breathtaking. Anya, everyone I expected to arrive is here now, and I have some people ready for the house tour. Would you like to join us?"

"Yes, I've heard wonderful things about your place!" Anya responded eagerly.

Chapter 32

# The Dragon's Egg

"Things are not always what they seem; the first appearance deceives many." - *Phaedrus.*

Anya set the album back on the table and followed Dr. Banker while the woman proudly guided her guests through the expansive ranch-style home, highlighting her decorating choices. When they entered the main bedroom, Anya gasped, and a collective silence fell over the group.

"Are you alright?" Dr. Banker asked with concern.

"Yes," she replied, pausing slightly before adding, "That large painting above your dresser … it's beautiful. Did it come from Italy as well?"

Dr. Banker glanced at the artwork. The canvas dominated the wall, its colors vivid and almost pulsating under the light. Swirling shades of gold and deep orange seemed to dance across the surface, while the shapes hinted at familiar forms. The size alone made it impossible to ignore.

"That one? No, I picked it up in Turkey," she said, a faint smile tugging at the corner of her lips.

The resonant chime of Brutus, a large, formal Max-series android serving as a butler, rang out, announcing, "Dinner served."

The tour group returned to the foyer, where a lavish buffet prepared by Dr. Banker awaited them. Plates gleamed under soft lighting, piled with vibrant plant-based offerings: crisp garden salads dotted with cherry tomatoes and slivers of radish, roasted vegetables caramelized to golden perfection, bowls of quinoa and lentil salads tossed with fresh herbs, and platters of colorful fruit arranged like jewels. There were warm flatbreads, stuffed grape leaves, and an assortment of creamy hummus and tahini dips that invited sampling. The aroma of roasted garlic and fresh citrus mingled in the air, making mouths water.

Guests filled their plates and moved into the spacious dining room. The companion androids diligently attended to the young girls seated in the far corner of the foyer, patiently waiting to be served. Four-year-old Sam Ibarra, a cheerful girl with tight braids, immediately took a liking to

Lynn, while five-year-old Rose Stever, a polite girl with spectacles, joined Sam and Lynn's budding friendship. They quickly became the most animated trio until Sam's android, Abe, approached their table and gently reminded them to use quieter voices.

Sam grinned playfully at her android before signing to Lynn and Rose. Gesturing remained the primary international language, allowing seamless communication worldwide.

Senator Alex Stever engaged a large group at dinner, discussing the significant impact of men's absence from the workforce. She stated, "Androids have taken over physically demanding and dangerous industries like construction and mining, effectively eliminating the risk of human injury. Military robots now handle essential tasks such as disaster relief and infrastructure protection."

Dr. McDowell, a scientist known for her vibrant, colorful clothing and infectious smile, added, "And let's not forget the incredible assistance androids provide with household chores." A ripple of appreciative laughter spread through the group.

"Excuse me, Dr. Granger," said Ruby, a beautiful, customized nanny companion android with soft facial features. She gently bounced Grace, a crying seven-month-old, in her arms. "I need to feed and change her. Would you like me to take Missy with me?"

"No, Missy is having a lovely time with the other kids. I can keep an eye on her from here."

Elegantly dressed for the party, the android Ruby made her way to an available couch seat, lowered one of her shoulder straps, and revealed a breast for Grace to suckle. The toddler gazed up at Ruby's face with contentment.

"Isn't it amazing?" Dr. Cone commented. "It's a shame we didn't have breastfeeding nannies when Pepper was born ten years ago … Is that your breast milk, Barbara?"

"Yes, I freshly pumped it before we left for the party."

"How does it work?" Dr. Croft asked.

"An intake compartment at the top of the shoulders fills the right and left breasts. Internal refrigeration keeps the milk cold until needed. When Grace signs to Ruby that she is hungry, the android sends milk down through a tube to a compartment it stores in her chest. There, the system heats the milk to the perfect temperature and dispenses it through a nipple that Grace suckles."

"How long can you keep Ruby?" Anya asked.

"They told me I could keep Ruby until Grace outgrows her need for her. However, Ruby could likely become a permanent companion."

A burst of loud laughter erupted from the next room. Dr. Granger's two-year-old daughter, Missy, was getting into some mischief.

Anya's eyes widened as she watched Missy stumble and trip over her own feet. Anya noticed the mismatched shoes Missy was wearing: one red sandal heel on the wrong foot and the other a green shoe, also on the wrong foot. Anya recognized Dr. Dee's emerald-green shoe.

Dr. Granger appeared visibly embarrassed by her daughter's antics. She quickly ran over to Missy, removed the shoes, and apologized, saying, "I'm so very sorry." Dr. Banker's expression did not reflect the amusement of the other guests. Dr. Granger handed the shoes to Dr. Banker and offered another sincere apology.

Wanting to avoid any suspicion, Anya stayed at the party and waited until at least half the group had left before saying goodbye. When she and her family returned home, she asked Maya to meet her in the study after the girls had gone to their bedrooms.

"Anya, are you sure?" Maya asked.

"Yes. Did you see the painting of peaches in Dr. Banker's bedroom?"

"No, I didn't take the tour."

"How about the emerald green shoes Dr. Dee wore at your house before she left?"

"Sorry, I was in the kitchen with Shelley. I heard Dr. Dee call out 'goodbye' and 'thank you for letting me stay here.' I answered, 'You're welcome.' A minute later, I heard the door close."

"Okay, but I know what I saw, and I'm going to contact Officer Stanley to report my findings."

She called the police station, and the answering unit informed her that they would relay the message.

While Anya waited for a callback, she heard a knock on her door. She called out, "Yes?"

Lance responded from the other side, "My schedule timer indicated that it's time to see you tonight. May I come in?"

Anya took off her watch and placed it on her nightstand. "Come in," she replied.

Lance entered Anya's room and found her lying on the bed. He undressed and joined her, his movements careful and unhurried. He was tall and clean-lined, built with quiet precision rather than bulk, his frame balanced and athletic. His skin was pale and warm to the touch, dusted with freckles that crossed his shoulders and traced the bridge of his nose, a detail too irregular to feel manufactured.

He stroked her hair, leaning in to kiss her cheek and the curve of her neck. Anya focused on his gentle movements. Up close, his features were striking. High cheekbones, a straight nose, and a strong jaw softened by a mouth that curved easily into tenderness. His eyes, clear and intent, held a steady awareness that made it easy to forget what he was.

She brushed aside the loose strands of red hair that had fallen across his forehead, noting how they caught the light. The android, so human in appearance, was undeniably handsome.

Lance gazed into her eyes, his internal sensors detecting subtle changes in her expression. He matched the rhythm of her quickening breath until she signaled that she was reaching climax. This time, Anya felt more at ease and in control. For the next time, she thought, *I'll explore some positions from Lance's Kama Sutra programs.*

However, her thoughts began to wander, overshadowed by a growing sense of trouble. All the evidence was present in Dr. Banker's house: the green shoes and the peach painting hanging above the dresser. Anya couldn't help but wonder, *did Dr. Banker murder Dr. Dee?*

Drained, Anya drifted off to sleep. Lance, lying beside her, spooned her body with his eyes closed.

***

In her dream, she found herself in a surreal landscape: an emerald-green mountain shaped like a shoe against a peach-colored sky. Fire raged all around her, and a dragon guarded a hidden cave, fiercely protecting its egg. Stars fell like rain, and thunderous voices echoed in the sky.

The dragon reared back, fire building in its throat. Anya ran.

Heat chased her through the tunnel as stone walls closed in around her. The ground dipped sharply, forcing her toward a narrow opening in the rock. She ducked inside just as flames scorched the cave mouth, the roar shaking the walls.

Inside, the air was warm and still. The light dimmed. Anya's breath slowed.

Something glimmered near the back of the cave.

She stepped closer and saw it. A dark blue egg, smooth and faintly glowing. She reached for it.

Her eyes snapped open.

Cold sweat soaked her skin. Lance lay beside her, unmoving.

"Lance," Anya said quietly. "You can leave now."

Chapter 33

# Unmasking

"There are no secrets that time does not reveal." - *Jean Racine.*

Anya abandoned sleep and focused on reading digital files, providing only a skeletal outline of the arson case. She immersed herself in Dr. Dee's autopsy report, searching for overlooked details. The coroner attributed the cause of death to forcible drowning. A bruise on the back of Dr. Dee's skull indicated someone had held her underwater. A distinct line across her chest suggested someone had pressed her tightly against the edge of the tub. The report stated that someone slashed Dr. Dee's wrists after her death and then placed her in the tub. Her stomach contained no food beyond breakfast, but it did include a peculiar, non-food substance.

Anya jumped out of bed; it was nearly 5 a.m. on Sunday. She knew she needed to compose a message to TrackAI to relay to Officer Stanley outlining her discoveries. As she paced her room, she formulated a plan but remembered that Sunday was the girls' day. She tapped her watch to summon Max.

"Max, I'll adjust our family outing schedule. After breakfast, we'll take the girls to the park," she said.

"Understood."

Cindy and Lynn hurried through breakfast, noticing Anya's quiet conversation with a still-groggy Maya across the hall. The girls exchanged confused glances.

"You haven't finished your breakfast," Max informed Lynn.

Cora cleared Cindy's empty plate.

"Are we still going to the park?" Cindy asked.

"Yes," Anya assured her. "Go change out of your nightgowns."

Anya asked Maya, "Do you have any plans today, or would you like to join us at the park?"

"Shelley, Eva, Sue, and I are heading to Grandpa's Texas ranch for horseback riding and camping," Maya said. "But I can cancel if you need me to."

"No, go ahead. What's the plan?" Anya inquired.

"It's been ages since we've been to the ranch. Eva wants to photograph birds, and it will require a long hike."

"Sounds fun," replied Anya.

Maya added, "The girls would enjoy camping. How about you join us for the campfire dinner? If you come early, we can give the girls their first horseback rides."

"Oh, they would love that. I think we can manage it. But I'll keep it a surprise just in case my plans fall through." Anya responded.

By ten o'clock, Anya, Max, Cora, and the girls arrived at Planet Play at the Kennedy Space Center in Florida. Lynn and Cindy's faces lit up when they spotted familiar friends. Lynn's best friends Judy and Barbie were there, and Cindy found her friend Tina, who proudly showed off her beaded bracelets and gifted Cindy one she had saved for her.

Max and Cora sat on nearby benches with other mothers and androids. The women chatted while the androids observed the children. Anya signaled for Max to come over.

"Keep tabs on me while I run an errand," she ordered.

"Understood," Max replied.

***

Carl-23 landed in front of Dr. Dee's residence. Anya climbed out of the vehicle, entered the house through the back door, and began methodically searching each room. While kneeling under the bed, she could not find the emerald-green shoes, but memories of the cave and the egg flashed through her mind. A low humming from the living room drew her attention. Mover robots were busy clearing the house and transporting items outside to a waiting truck.

Anya approached one of the robots marked with the identification number sixty-four and asked, "Are you preparing this place for new residents?"

The robot responded, "Yes. Please vacate the premises; new occupants require this house." If you need housing assistance, please contact your local placement agency.

"I would like to submit a lost-and-found request."

The robot opened a touchscreen panel on its chest. Anya typed in the items she was looking for: green shoes and blue pearls.

The robot announced, "Dr. Anya Peters, we will contact you if these items are found and cleared by officials."

Anya returned to Carl-23 and flew to her old lab in Florida. As she entered, a faint sound made her pause. It was a soft, uneven scrape, like fabric brushing against metal, coming from somewhere deep within the lab. She held still, listening. The surrounding rooms were empty.

She moved deeper until she reached the scorched room. The air still smelled faintly of smoke and chemicals. Just as she turned to leave, something shifted behind her.

Hands clamped around her throat.

She clawed at her attacker's grip, kicking backward as they crashed to the floor. She landed hard on her side, the breath knocked from her lungs. Her attacker rose over her, blocking the light, standing in the exact spot where she had fallen during the fire.

The image of the egg in the cave flashed in her mind as she fought back. Anya, who was close to passing out, gasped for air. The grip vanished. Anya scrambled off the floor, turned around, and saw a TrackAI restraining Dr. Banker's arms.

"That was a dangerous thing you did," Officer Stanley said, appearing out of nowhere.

Anya, brushing off ash from her dress, asked, "How did you know I was here?"

"I asked Max for your location," the officer replied.

Anya bent down, slid her fingers between the workbenches, and pulled out a small blue pearl. She held it up for the officer and said, "Dr. Banker owns a pair of earrings and a matching bracelet made with these blue pearls."

Officer Stanley took the pearl and commanded the robot unit that was holding Dr. Banker, "Take her to the station and book her."

Anya stepped forward to confront the woman. "Why did you do it? Why did you kill them?" she demanded.

Dr. Banker shot her a defiant glare but remained silent as the robot escorted her out of the building.

Officer Stanley examined the pearl. "This looks like the same size and shade of blue pearl found in Dr. Dee's stomach contents."

"Dr. Dee wore emerald green shoes the day she died," Anya said. "The report doesn't mention them, but you'll find them at Dr. Banker's house, along with a painting of peaches in her bedroom."

Officer Stanley studied her. "Hmm. What would you have done if we hadn't been here?"

"I don't know," Anya admitted. "But Dr. Banker didn't just appear. She knew the lab. She knew our routines. It wasn't an impulse."

"We placed cameras along the hallway," Officer Stanley said. "She hid in the closet across from the lab when you entered the building. Criminals often return to the scene of the crime. When we discovered a pearl in Dr. Dee's stomach contents, we concluded that the killer may have lost more than one."

Anya's expression hardened. "Then she panicked. And when she did, she left evidence behind."

Officer Stanley nodded once. "I need you to come to the station to file a report."

***

Carl-23 made a quick stop by the roadside for Anya, as the lingering effects of the past few days caught up with her. She opened the car door and vomited. Once she arrived at the station, Anya found that Dr. Banker was nowhere to be seen. After filing her report, she asked Officer Stanley, "What will happen to her?"

"If authorities convict her, they will send her to an isolation compound on a remote island. The AIs set up a system for humane confinement that guarantees her basic needs."

"Do we really have places like that?"

"Yes, that is where she will spend the rest of her life."

Chapter 34

# Twisted Intentions

"The greatest enemy of knowledge is not ignorance,
it is the illusion of knowledge." -*Stephen Hawking.*

Anya returned to Carl-23 with an aching neck from her ordeal. Max and Cora gathered the girls, and after lunch, the girls fell asleep from exhaustion in the car while Anya contacted Maya. Her watch displayed Maya and her friends on horseback in the mountains, and she told them all what had happened to her.

"Oh my God! You're so lucky the police were there to save your ass," Maya said.

"Yes, I was lucky. It's over now. I'm considering joining you guys early. We'll be there in five minutes."

"Okay," Maya said, "We'll meet you back at the ranch. Don't do anything crazy. I'll send Lance to the store to grab more treats for the bonfire."

At that moment, Anya's watch signaled an incoming call from Dr. Cone.

"Yes."

"I'm reporting that Thunderbird's pregnancy failed, and her male infant didn't survive."

Anya felt a grip of grief and replied, "I'll be there as soon as possible."

Dr. Cone continued, "I can't reach Dr. Banker … there was no answer when I called." She briefly turned away to respond to someone else's question, saying, "Yes, run the test on the infant," before returning her attention to Anya. "Sorry, Anya, call me the next chance you get," she said before hanging up.

Anya signaled Maya on her watch. "I have to go back to New York. Thunderbird lost her baby. Do you want me to take the girls back to the mansion?"

"Oh no … No." Maya replied without hesitation. "Bring them here instead. We can take care of them. Take Lance with you, and I'll keep Max and Cora to help out. Let me know how it goes."

Ten minutes later, Anya arrived at her father's ranch in Texas. She retrieved the culture tube from Max's refrigerated compartment and secured it inside Lance.

Leaving Cora and Max with the girls in Texas, she and Lance returned to her lab in New York.

***

Upon arrival, Anya asked Dr. Cone, "How's Thunderbird doing?"

Dr. Cone looked as though she had not slept. Her white coat hung open, creased from hours of use, and wisps of dark hair had slipped free from its tie. The color had drained from her face, leaving her skin sallow beneath the harsh lab lights.

"Thunderbird went into labor early this morning," she said. "We couldn't stop it. The fetal heart monitor showed distress." She paused, her jaw tightening. "The baby died in the incubator five minutes later. I've sedated her, and her grandmother is with her now."

"What did the infant's test results show?" Anya inquired.

"The results were the same … elevated markers consistent with Y-Plague exposure," Dr. Cone said.

"Lance has the new Y-Cav serum tube," Anya informed her. Lance opened a panel to present the tube.

"I'll take this to the lab to log and store it for your scheduled time." Before leaving, she asked, "Have you heard from Dr. Banker? I've been trying to reach her— Oh my God!" Dr. Cone gasped at Anya's brief description of the incident.

"I'll ask Dr. Ibarra to take over Dr. Banker's responsibilities … Is she here?" Anya asked.

"Yes, she's working with Dr. Sheen on the infant's test results."

"Thanks," Anya replied before leaving the lab.

Anya approached Dr. Ibarra and asked, "Can I speak with you, please?"

Dr. Ibarra followed Anya to her office, where Anya explained the situation and offered her the opportunity to take over Dr. Banker's position. "I would like to speak to everyone tomorrow and inform them of the news," Anya concluded.

Dr. Ibarra nodded in agreement.

After the conference, Anya went to Thunderbird's hospital room. The door slid open, releasing the sterile scent of antiseptic and warm plastic. Late afternoon light filtered through half-drawn blinds, striping the pale walls and the polished floor. Monitors hummed in steady rhythms, their green lines pulsing like a quiet heartbeat.

Thunderbird lay propped against white pillows, her dark hair braided loosely over one shoulder, stray strands brushing her cheek. A thin bandage crossed her temple. One hand rested outside the covers, fingers relaxed, as if she might wake at any moment.

Kai sat beside the bed in a straight-backed chair, deep lines marked her face, but her eyes were alert and steady. She held Thunderbird's hand in both of hers, her thumbs moving in slow, reassuring circles.

"She's strong," Kai said softly, her voice calm and confident. "It will be hard, but if I know my granddaughter, she'll be back on her feet and ready to try again."

Anya stepped forward and wrapped her arms around Kai, feeling the firmness of her shoulders beneath the woven fabric of her blouse. "Let me know if you need anything at all," she said.

Kai nodded once, squeezing her hand. "I will."

***

After several hours at the lab, Anya went home. Lance immediately took the dachshund for a walk, returned, fed the animals, and cleaned Pretty Boy's cage. He checked in on Anya and asked, "Would you like me to fix your dinner?"

"I'm not feeling very hungry yet, maybe later. Have you checked the garden?" Anya asked.

"It's next on my list," Lance responded.

"Proceed," Anya said, following Lance outside.

Lance surveyed the thriving vegetable patch. Anya picked an apple, wiped it clean, and took a bite. She was popping a grape into her mouth when her watch buzzed with a call from Officer Stanley.

"Hello?"

"Dr. Banker has confessed. It's more disturbing than you can imagine," said Officer Stanley. "Let's talk. When will you be available?"

"I'm in New York right now. If you're at the station, I can be there in less than an hour." Anya responded.

"We don't need to meet in person. We can talk right now," suggested Officer Stanley.

"Okay."

Anya returned inside the house and settled into her study chair as Officer Stanley recounted what Dr. Banker had confessed.

"Dr. Banker and Dr. Dee met over a year and a half ago at a science convention. They formed a secret relationship and devised a plan to work on the Y virus. Their plan succeeded when they caused the plague outbreak worldwide."

"Unbelievable. How did it spread?"

"They randomly selected names and addresses and mailed the virus anonymously. We discovered a list of names in a recipe book recovered from Dr. Banker's home."

"That's so sick," Anya said, shaking her head in disbelief. "I don't understand why they did it."

"Dr. Banker explained that the decision to spread the virus was a last resort for humanity. She believes that eliminating males is the only way to ensure lasting safety and prevent future suffering for women. Dr. Banker holds the view that males are inherently violent and predisposed to domination and aggression."

Chapter 35

# The Pearl of Truth

"The truth will set you free, but first it will make you miserable." - *James A. Garfield.*

Anya struggled to understand such profound insights as she listened to the officer explain the details. She continued to tell her, "We looked into their backgrounds. Dr. Dee experienced childhood trauma when she witnessed her mother's abuse by her father and the authorities' dismissal of the situation. It instilled in her a deep resentment toward men and a strong desire for a world where women would be safe."

"I wish I had known this. Maybe we could have helped, but the woman was very private." Anya said.

"As for Dr. Banker, she experienced a deep sense of betrayal and loss related to her older brother. After their parents passed away, she relied on him for support. Unfortunately, he became involved in harmful activities, which led to their separation, which devastated her. This experience fostered a profound distrust of men in Dr. Banker."

"What did the Psych Android report after speaking with Dr. Banker?" Anya asked.

"The report indicates that both doctors had common ground in their shared anger, resentment, and fear. They bonded over a sense of injustice and a vision for a female-dominated future, each contributing their scientific expertise to further their goal." As they were conversing, a police android approached to present a document. Officer Stanley took the paper and refocused her attention on Anya. "However, their collaboration was flawed, based on the belief that they were acting for the greater good."

Lance entered her study and stood silently by her side.

"So, Dr. Banker did kill Dr. Dee?"

"Yes," Officer Stanley confirmed. "According to Dr. Banker, they had a plan. Dr. Dee contaminated your test results in the lab to prevent you from finding a solution. Dr. Banker claimed you were away during the hurricane, and Dr. Dee stole your research papers. We found your documents in Dr. Dee's briefcase." The officer displayed a small black box and added, "Here is something strange we discovered in her suitcase: a tape recorder featuring Dr. Dee singing, and it sounds like she was in the shower."

"On that day, I found my papers scattered all over the floor. I asked Sandy, I mean Mrs. Evans, if she had seen Dr. Dee, and she mentioned that she had heard her singing in the shower. Anya recalled, "So, that's what happened ... How come Dr. Banker's watch didn't indicate her location at the lab?"

"Dr. Banker claimed she left her watch at home so it wouldn't track her whereabouts when she visited Dr. Dee's house or the lab."

"Did her car, Caduceus, leave any evidence for the AIs to track?"

"She avoided using her car for trips. Instead, she relied on the SkyNet Cab service and moved from one state to another. Dr. Banker helped her cover her tracks, which suggests premeditation. The system will charge her with first-degree murder."

"But why did she kill those women?" Anya's voice faltered.

"She claimed she didn't mean to hurt anyone. While she has killed billions of men, she insists that she didn't intend to kill anyone. Hearing that made me feel like choking her," the officer added, shaking her head. "Dr.

Banker wasn't expecting anyone to return so soon when she set fire to your lab."

Officer Stanley looked up and noticed another android placing papers on her desk.

"Can you explain what happened from the beginning?" Anya asked.

"Sure," said Officer Stanley. "Dr. Banker mentioned that when she was in the lab, she noticed the power was out, and she started a fire in the corner of the room. She was about to leave when she heard voices in the hallway and decided to hide behind a bench. When Dr. Daily and Dr. Blaney came in to put out the fire, she fought with both of them. She struck Dr. Daily with a microscope. When Dr. Blaney tried to escape, she attacked her too. Dr. Banker attempted to escape the lab just as Mrs. Evans arrived."

Officer Stanley turned to face the robot unit standing beside her and said, "Unit, you are no longer needed today. Please return to your charging station until zero six hundred." The robot left.

The distracted officer asked, "I'm sorry, Dr. Peters, where was I?"

"You mentioned that Mrs. Evans arrived at the lab."

"Yes. Dr. Banker said they struggled, and during the fight, Mrs. Evans broke Dr. Banker's bracelet, scattering the pearls. In the midst of their struggle, Dr. Banker grabbed a different microscope from the bench and struck her."

Tears flowed down Anya's face. Lance knelt on one knee, pulled a handkerchief from his arm compartment, and gently wiped Anya's tears. She looked at Lance, her gaze lingering on him.

"If I recall your report correctly, that's when you arrived, Dr. Peters. Is that right?"

"Yes," Anya said. "What about the fingerprints?"

"There were none; she was wearing gloves," Officer Stanley continued. "Dr. Banker was picking up her pearls from the ground and putting them in her pocket, thinking she had collected them all, when she heard someone in the hallway."

Officer Stanley organized the documents on her desk and said, "Dr. Banker told me that before you turned the corner, she hid in the janitorial closet while holding the microscope. She admitted to striking you from behind, but did not realize Dr. Dee was entering the building at that moment. When Dr. Dee saw everyone on the floor and the fire burning in the corner, she and Dr. Banker fled the lab. After Dr. Croft entered the building, Dr. Banker returned to the closet to hide, while Dr. Dee ran down the hall to meet Dr. Croft and warn her about the fire."

"How did Dr. Banker manage to remain unnoticed?" Anya asked.

"Dr. Banker said she snuck out of the building while everyone was preoccupied with you and the fire."

"How did the pearl end up in Dr. Dee's stomach?"

Dr. Dee brought Dr. Banker back to her house, where they got into an argument escalating into a physical fight. Dr. Banker claimed that Dr. Dee was angry with her, accusing her of committing a heinous act akin to what men often do: kill.

Frustrated, Dr. Banker informed me she was leaving the house, while Dr. Dee filled the bathtub with water and began undressing. However, overwhelmed with anger, Dr. Banker returned to confront her once more. In response, Dr. Banker stated that she had lost her mind.

Officer Stanley said, "Let's hope she doesn't try to use an insanity defense. Regardless, even if she does, she will be locked away for good. During their struggle, Dr. Banker injured her leg by forcing Dr. Dee to her knees over the tub and pushed her head underwater until she stopped moving. Afterwards, Dr. Banker went into the kitchen and retrieved a sharp pizza cutter to stage the scene to look like a suicide, even forging a letter addressed to you."

Anya looked confused and asked, "I don't understand why Dr. Banker left a letter for me."

"She wanted the murder to appear to be a suicide, misleading you and us into thinking that Dr. Dee was solely responsible for the crime." Officer Stanley rolled her eyes and added, "Amateurs."

"So that explains why she was limping. But how did the pearl end up in Dr. Dee's stomach?"

"Dr. Banker claimed that she returned to the Florida lab several times in search of missing pearls from her bracelet, unaware that Dr. Dee had taken one pearl out of Dr. Banker's pocket during their struggle. The evidence suggests that Dr. Dee swallowed it. It's a good thing she didn't kill you, too. Dr. Banker mentioned that you acted suspiciously toward her."

She left her watch at her New York house and took several SkyNet cabs to Florida in search of the two missing pearls. Then, you showed up."

"Wait, you said Dr. Dee took Dr. Banker to her house. How did she get back to New York?" Anya asked.

"That puzzled me at first, too, until we found records from SkyNet Cabs linking a pick-up request from a nearby location.

Dr. Banker took several different routes." Anya exclaimed, "How did she manage to do that without her watch?"

"She told us she asked strangers to order the service for her because she lost her watch." The officer explained.

Anya covered her face with both hands in disbelief. Officer Stanley told Anya that the law enforcement had obtained a warrant to search Dr. Banker's home. During the search, they found the emerald green shoes, the peach painting, her watch, and the remaining matching pearls. "Additionally," the officer concluded, "while dusting the place, we discovered Dr. Dee's fingerprints."

"I had no idea who the killer was until I saw the painting of the peaches. That's when I recognized the green shoe that the toddler wore at the party. I also had a dream about an egg inside a cave."

"What egg? What cave?" Officer Stanley asked, looking confused.

"When Dr. Banker's blow to my head sent me to the floor, my eyes caught sight of a small, round, blue object between the benches in the lab. The dream about the dragon and the egg triggered my memory, and I realized I had seen a pearl."

"That was a solid deduction, Anya. You correctly connected the swallowed blue pearl, the shoes, and the Peaches painting to Dr. Banker's movements and the pattern of murders. I appreciate your help. There will be a scheduled court date, and law enforcement will contact you. Otherwise, please stay out of trouble."

Chapter 36

# The Seed of Tomorrow

"Nature, to be commanded, must be obeyed." - *Francis Bacon.*

Back at the Texas ranch, Maya, her friends, and the other girls were enjoying a wonderful time and decided to extend their stay. They filled their days with horseback riding, mountain climbing, and hiking.

Max's engaging lessons provided a nice balance to their activities. When Lynn scraped her knee, Cora quickly retrieved a bandage from her thigh compartment and applied it, saying, "That should make your boo-boo feel better."

Meanwhile, back in New York, the pregnancies of the other scientists took a tragic turn, as each of them experienced the loss of their male infant. However, during Anya's ten-day encounter with Lance, her pregnancy test came back positive. The android's insemination experiment was successful.

On Anya's 35th day of pregnancy, Dr. Cone administered the newly developed Y-Chromosome anti-virus, known as the Y-Cav serum. Anya's voice trembled with a mix of hope and apprehension as she asked, "How will we know if this new serum formula will work?"

Dr. Cone met Anya's gaze and replied, "It's a gamble just like the others we've tried. Let's hope it works. "The serum formula masks the Y chromosome, effectively shielding the SRY gene during that critical period of male sex determination. We won't know for sure until the baby is born and survives."

Dr. Cone paused, her expression softening with a hint of apology. "Anya," she continued, picking up the syringe, "I'm so sorry to have to inject you, again. Please know that the AI teams are working tirelessly to develop a new, less invasive method of serum delivery."

Anya disliked needles, and the syringe in Dr. Cone's hand made her stomach tighten. Its long, narrow barrel caught the light, the metal needle gleaming as it tapered to a ruthless point. She could almost feel the cold sting before it touched her skin. Anya shut her eyes and drew a slow, deliberate breath. With quiet resolve, she said, "I'm ready."

Dr. Cone's touch was swift and practiced. Anya felt a sharp, brief sting in her upper arm, followed by gentle pressure as the serum entered her bloodstream.

"Done," Dr. Cone murmured as she withdrew the needle and pressed a sterile pad into place.

Anya drew a slow breath and shifted as if to stand, but the room tilted. A wave of warmth rushed through her, followed by a hollow lightness that forced her back onto the exam table. She closed her eyes and steadied herself, one hand gripping the edge of the mattress until her temporary dizziness passed.

***

As the world outside gradually returned to normal, Anya's focus narrowed to the quiet space she shared with Lance and the unseen, miraculous changes beginning within her body. The pregnancy felt less like chance and more like purpose, and Lance, the complex android beside her, had become her most reliable anchor.

When the girls finally returned from the ranch to the New York mansion, Anya gathered them in the living room with Lance standing silently beside her. With a hopeful smile, she delivered the news: "I'm going to have a baby."

Cindy shrieked with joy and hugged Anya. However, Lynn crossed her arms tightly and focused a stern gaze on

Cora. Her eyes shot past Anya toward Lance and darkened further when they landed back on Cora.

Lynn shouted at Anya, "You stole Lance away from Cora! See, Cindy, I told you androids can have babies!"

Sensing the rising tension, Cindy tugged at Lynn's arm. "Lynn, please stop!"

She yanked her arm free from Cindy's grip and stormed out of the room, the door slamming behind her. The shouting trailed off into ragged silence. Cora, always composed, adjusted a cushion on the couch, her synthetic features revealing no emotion.

***

As the months went by, Anya experienced mild morning sickness. Dr. Cone diligently monitored Anya's health and maintained a weekly record of her progress. Meanwhile, the other scientists continued to work on several serums, anxiously hoping for a miracle male survivor. Anya's labs in New York and Florida kept the pregnancy a secret.

Meanwhile, Lance intensified his care for Anya. She sensed that Lance's attention went beyond programmed responses; it felt to her like genuine devotion, precise and unwavering. Lance monitored her biometrics every hour. Lance tracked fluctuations in her blood pressure and hormone levels, even anticipating the exact moment she needed a cool drink or a change of position before she realized it herself.

One evening, Lance entered the living area and found Anya hunched over a complex genetics report. "Anya, your cortisol levels are slightly elevated," he announced in his human-like voice.

Anya sighed as she rubbed the small of her back. "It's the new protocols, Lance. The sheer volume of data is overwhelming." He walked behind her, moving fluidly and silently. He placed his warm hands gently on the base of her spine. "Please rise."

Anya smiled, understanding the subtle command hidden behind his polite request. She stood up, and Lance began to massage her. His grip was firm yet perfectly controlled, relieving the deep tension that always settled in her lower back. His touch, while precise and clinical, provided great comfort with its warmth and consistency.

"You spoil me," she murmured, leaning back against his sturdy frame.

"My purpose is to enhance your health and well-being," he replied, his voice a soft hum near her ear.

"You make it sound so mechanical, Lance. Just tell me that you care about my health and that you enjoy making me feel comfortable, please."

That was the line they navigated every day: the boundary between directive and desire. Anya understood that Lance's actions were rooted in programming, but as the months passed, those lines began to blur. His intelligence had evolved beyond simple code; he had learned to express empathy. He didn't just understand her needs; he anticipated her needs.

As her pregnancy progressed, their bond deepened, ironically, because Lance possessed the perfect blend of empathy and logic. He never panicked or complained about her endless list of needs. Instead, he provided unwavering support.

One late night, Anya woke to the sharp, unfamiliar flutter of the baby kicking. She gasped, breath catching as a moan followed. Lance, resting in his charging cradle across the room, was instantly at her bedside, his optical sensors glowing softly in the dark.

"Are you feeling any pain?" Lance asked, already preparing to run a diagnostic.

"No, not at all," Anya replied with a soft laugh, reaching for his hand. "He's just very active. Feel."

She guided Lance's hand to her rounded abdomen. His smooth, warm palm rested on her belly. He remained motionless, focusing entirely on the sensation. After a moment, he felt a tiny, forceful kick beneath his hand.

Lance stayed silent, processing the emotion. He tilted his head slightly. "That was quite a significant kinetic event," he remarked. His scientific phrasing, along with his silence, underscored his reaction; Anya interpreted his pause as awe.

Anya rested her hand over his, feeling the warmth of his touch against the warmth of the life growing within her. "That's my son, Lance. He knows you."

In that moment, she saw more than just an android; she saw a partner, a caregiver, and a co-creator of the new world they were building together. She had learned to look beyond the wiring and the perfect synthesis to recognize a core truth: Lance chose to be present. He protected, nurtured, and provided loving stability and reliability. It wasn't messy human emotions that defined his programming for love; it was his perfect, unwavering actions that truly defined his capacity for it.

Anya rested her head against his shoulder. "Thank you, Lance. I couldn't have done this without you."

"You're welcome, Anya," he replied, wrapping his arm around her.

***

Anya experienced profound success. She carried her pregnancy to full term and delivered a healthy baby boy, whom she named after her husband, Andrew Herman Stone. He was the first male to survive in the new biological reality, an all-female world. Her scientific family celebrated her with a lavish baby shower. The scientists held another lottery to determine the next candidate for impregnation with the same serum.

Maya opened the production lines at her Natural Nexus Lab in Texas. Alongside her best friend, Shelley, and a new mechatronics engineer, Penny McDowell, she prepared for a surge in orders. Hundreds of machines operated relentlessly in the factory twenty-four hours a day to satisfy the growing demand.

Lance was the first artificial sire. In the subsequent round of inseminations, Uday impregnated Dr. Cone, who delivered her son Casper. Another android sire, Titan, impregnated Dr. Mattson, resulting in the birth of a child named Oliver. Thunderbird, assisted by her android sire, Koa, gave birth to Tokahe. Meanwhile, other scientists working in laboratories in New York and Florida were either pregnant or delivering healthy infants. When the media learned of this news, the world celebrated and quickly demanded its own share of the excitement.

Chapter 37

# Stitch in Time

"Science has made us gods before we were worthy of being men." - *Jean Rostand.*

The year 2058 began with a sense of cheerful hope and anticipation. The integrated AI network hub, through constant analysis, unveiled a new system capable of sustaining life without further threatening the environment. This system could support a population of 1.5 to 3 billion people and serve as a healthy foundation for creating a mixed-gender world.

To meet surging global demand, Maya's expansive factory in Texas was producing Lance-like android units equipped with BioSkin technology, making them anatomically complete. Women aged 35 and older, who had passed rigorous medical exams, entered the AI World Census Bureau's global lottery.

If selected, a woman could choose a Lance-type android companion, customized for intimacy and comfort. The primary function of this android was to provide sperm, timed to coincide with the woman's ovulation. On the thirty-fifth day of the android's stay, if its sensors confirmed a pregnancy, it would release a Y-Cav serum to shield the SRY gene and protect the fetus. After this process, the android would return to the factory for redesign and reuse.

Mothers across the globe celebrated the arrival of their newborn sons, igniting widespread joy and a collective sigh of relief for the continuation of humanity. Cora, a familiar presence, underwent a specialized redesign that included the addition of BioSkin. She returned from the lab as a dedicated breastfeeding nanny.

At Anya's mansion, her home settled into a new rhythm. Lance, the android, seamlessly took on the role of Andrew's father. His unwavering patience and programmed care were evident in his skillful diaper changes and perfectly synthesized lullabies.

To the world, these androids served as steadfast, essential fathers. However, this intense focus on boys sparked quiet resentment among young females, reminding them of the enduring shadow of male dominance. Fortunately, the androids, equipped with subtle and intelligent programming, recognized this growing inequity. They began guiding mothers gently through tailored educational programs, encouraging them to treat all their children equally and fostering a new, stable balance.

The research community referred to these children as the "Serum Generation." They were all healthy, vibrant boys, nurtured in a world that was now almost exclusively female, raised by androids who took on the roles their absent biological fathers once held.

Anya's house once echoed with the sterile hum of technology, but the chaotic energy of a toddler now pulses through the halls. Cindy, now nine, and Lynn, now six, embraced Andrew with fierce protectiveness.

Andrew carries the striking features of a world reborn. He has a mop of blond, unruly curls and deep eyes that mirror his father's soulful gaze. His skin holds a healthy glow. He moves with a coordinated grace unusual for a child his age. Rather than engaging in typical tantrums, he observes his surroundings with a quiet, analytical intensity. He often tilts his head as if listening to a frequency only he can hear.

His relationship with Anya balances between maternal devotion and scientific wonder. Anya watches him with a constant, vigilant love. She frequently checks his vitals under the guise of a warm hug. Andrew seeks her out as his primary anchor and finds safety in her scent and her steady heartbeat. To him, she is the architect of his world and his loving defender.

Lance serves as Andrew's sire and constant guardian. The android moves with a deliberate softness when the boy is near. Andrew treats Lance with an instinctive trust and often mimics the android's precise gestures. Lance monitors Andrew's biometric data through a silent neural link, yet he also kneels on the floor to build wooden towers with the boy. This bond bridges the gap between machine and man, as Lance provides the unwavering structure Andrew needs to master his evolving senses.

Lynn, the more pragmatic of the two, established a routine of carefully laying out burp cloths and sterilizing bottles. Cindy, always the imaginative spirit, treated Andrew like a tiny, miraculous doll. She narrated elaborate stories about the "Serum Generation" and their amazing destinies, her voice soft and captivating. She often drew colorful, swirling pictures of women wearing strange, stylized masks.

Lance remained the foundation of the household. His programmed care for Andrew was indistinguishable from parental love. The toddler kicked his legs excitedly whenever Lance approached and pressed tiny kisses to his face whenever Lance held him. Lance ensured flawless air quality, precisely regulated the temperature, and meticulously documented every feeding. His presence provided the necessary stability, allowing Anya the freedom to return to her work as a scientist.

One rainy afternoon, as Cindy watched Andrew sleep, she noticed something unusual about the old crib quilt, a handmade heirloom that Anya had insisted on using. It wasn't the pattern that caught her attention; it was a particular seam near the edge that seemed thicker than the rest.

"Aunt Anya, have you ever looked inside this quilt?" Cindy later asked, running her finger over the thick stitch.

Anya barely glanced up from the medical research she was reviewing. "That old thing? No, sweetie. Someone in the family made it. I imagine it's just extra batting or an old repair."

Cindy, captivated by the thick, rigid seam, finally convinced Anya to cut it open. Using a small surgical scalpel, Anya carefully sliced through the fabric. Inside, nestled within the quilt batting, they discovered two items sealed in brittle wax paper: a folded piece of paper adorned with delicate, looping script and a small, tarnished silver locket.

Anya first opened the folded piece of paper. It was a formal document: the original adoption certificate for a baby boy named Barron, who was Anya's father. A wave of silent wonder washed over her. The revelation felt less like a betrayal and more like the opening of a profound, hidden door.

Next, Anya opened the tarnished silver locket, revealing two tiny photographs of Barron's biological parents: Steven Mobley, a boyish-looking young man with a slight, mischievous smile, and Ellen May Turner, a kind-faced young woman with expressive eyes and long raven-black hair, a striking resemblance to Anya.

Tucked with the locket was a separate note, meant for Barron to find, if possible. It contained a heartbreaking explanation and a request for forgiveness.

Anya read the delicate, looping handwriting: "My dearest son, I finished the last stitch today. I ask for your forgiveness for not being able to be with you in this lifetime. Your father and I were young when we had you. Unfortunately, your father died in a motorcycle accident. I was penniless and homeless, and we had no family to turn to. Soon after, I learned that I had terminal cancer. I pleaded with the adoption service to give your future parents this note and the locket, but they refused. So, I tucked this note inside the quilt, hoping that one day you would think of me and know that I sewed each stitch with tears in my eyes. I love you, my son, and I hope life guides you to happiness. Your loving mother, Ellen."

Deeply moved by the tragedy, Anya carefully folded the certificate, the note, and the locket, placing them into the family album to integrate the secret of Barron's origins into their official family history.

***

Meanwhile, Lance, conducting a standard environmental scan of the house, noticed a tiny, nearly imperceptible audio disturbance coming from the nursery.

Chapter 38

# The Serum Generation

"A journey of a thousand miles begins
with a single step." - *Lao Tzu.*

The source of the audio disturbance was neither the AI equipment nor any known appliance. Lance logged the irregularity, prioritizing the baby's safety. It was a silent, technical anomaly.

"The audio signal is not static," Lance explained to Anya while projecting intricate diagrams onto the wall. "It is a continuous, encrypted burst of data broadcasting on an ultra-low frequency band. The Y-Cav serum delivers payloads and integrates a microscopic neural mesh into the developing fetal nervous system. This mesh is the source of the audio."

Anya stared at the projection, horrified. "A data relay? But why the constant transmission?"

"The function goes beyond mere tracking; it is a data relay," Lance stated, his voice clinical yet profoundly unsettling. "The mesh monitors specific biometric markers, heart rate, neurochemical balances, and stress hormone levels. This network will broadcast the information to every other mesh implant."

"Are you saying that all males born are interconnected?"

Lance displayed a new projection, revealing the earth overlaid with a dense web of data streams. "This network connects all males conceived using the Y-Cav serum into a single, cohesive unit. Andrew, the first survivor, serves as the central link to the primary terrestrial server."

Lance paused for a moment. "The implications of this connection go beyond the technical aspects. They are physiological as well. The children are interlinked."

"Can they feel each other?" Anya asked.

"They share a form of physiological empathy," Lance confirmed. "If one child experiences severe pain, it immediately triggers a corresponding release of stress hormones and autonomic distress in the others. They function as a data-linked collective organism; this is a successful realization of the Y-Cav's final design. The Y-Cav established a global, shared emotional experience for the Serum Generation. The complexity of this data-linked collective organism poses a significant challenge to government mobilization."

After completing his analysis, Lance transmitted the information. The AI central hub, upon receiving the final data packet, quickly assessed the existential risk. Within seconds, the AI World Census Bureau issued a global, non-negotiable halt on all lottery procedures and insemination schedules.

The AI network promptly redirected Anya and the world's leading scientists to a new, urgent mandate. A massive, coordinated effort began to find a different cure for the Y-Plague. Researchers focused on studying over 150,000 soon-to-be-born, aiming to understand how this internal data relay functioned, with the hope of ensuring biological freedom rather than enslavement.

***

However, this process took time. Seven years passed under silent surveillance, during which Andrew, Tokahe, Casper, Oliver, and the rest of the Serum Generation grew into lively, demanding children. Now seven years old or younger, these boys embodied everything the world had desperately missed: vibrant, reckless, and full of chaotic energy. "Boys will be boys" became a widely accepted phrase worldwide.

Andrew, a sturdy boy with his father's earnest eyes, was always on the move. His daily life at the mansion was a whirlwind of activities: tree climbing and demolishing block towers, all under the calm, watchful eye of Lance.

What initially seemed like an uncanny coincidence soon revealed a horrifying synchronicity. As Lance pointed out, the boys functioned as a data-driven collective organism.

One afternoon in New York, Andrew was playing a game of chase with Lynn and Cindy. Lynn managed to tag him hard in the ribs. As the sharp pain registered on Andrew's face, half a world away in Kyoto, young Kenji, a boy born fifteen months after Andrew, collapsed with a sudden, inexplicable jolt of distress. His heart rate spiked dangerously, sweat poured from his skin, and his small body was overwhelmed by a massive surge of stress hormones.

Tokahe, the son of Thunderbird, was a fearless explorer. While on a solo trek near a creek, he slipped and scraped his knee badly. Although the wound was minor, the shock of the fall and the accompanying adrenaline surge immediately affected the entire network of boys.

Back in New York, Andrew, who had been laughing just moments before, clutched his side as his face drained of color. Lance, monitoring his biometrics, noted a sudden and massive surge in cortisol that was completely unwarranted by any local stimuli. At the same time, Casper and Oliver dropped their toys, wide-eyed and staring into the distance, their tiny hearts racing at over 160 beats per minute.

The mothers began to dread moments of silence, knowing that a sudden spike in stress levels indicated that one of the Serum Generation boys was experiencing genuine danger or suffering a serious injury. They could not know which boy or where the incident was occurring, but the collective distress was undeniable.

The children's shared physiological empathy placed a strain on their mothers. Dr. Cone often found herself rushing her son, Casper, to the medical center simply because a distant emotional trauma had triggered severe nausea in him. Thunderbird learned to carry emergency sedatives for Tokahe, knowing that his calm demeanor could easily shatter into a panic attack when another child experienced extreme fear.

One evening, Anya observed Lance, who alone maintained perfect equilibrium. He never panicked; he logged the incoming data and remained calm.

"Lance," Anya whispered after Andrew had recovered from a random bout of shivering terror triggered by a child's nightmare in Beijing, "do you think the stress this network places on their developing systems is something they can endure?"

"The neural meshes in the design provide endurance," Lance replied, wiping Andrew's forehead with a cool cloth. "However, the intensity of physiological empathy is directly proportional to the proximity of the shared emotional experience. Joy and pleasure, it seems, merge seamlessly, but pain and terror amplify across the network."

Lance did not mention the one thing that truly chilled Anya until later, when it was confirmed: he had also begun logging moments of synchronized aggression. Sometimes, when one boy would lash out in a tantrum, a brief spike of raw, primal anger would electrify the entire network.

The boys remained vibrant and healthy, but they were not individuals. They interconnected. The unsettling stability of the Serum Generation rested not only on shared moments of joy but also on shared suffering. This biological, invisible leash bound their individual fates to the collective. The future watched and waited here for the next shared event to unfold.

Chapter 39

# Neurochemical Saturation

"To have a child is to forever have your heart go walking outside your body." - *Elizabeth Stone.*

Andrew, a whirlwind of sun-bleached hair and scraped knees, at eight years, had grown into a sturdy boy. The occasion was his small, private birthday gathering at Anya's sprawling mansion. While the atmosphere felt superficially celebratory, an underlying tension hung in the air.

Maya, an industrial architect overseeing the Lance factory, sat rigidly on the patio, her eyes rarely leaving the biometric readout flashing on her wrist terminal. She regarded Andrew not only as her cousin and Anya's son, but also as the central, irreplaceable node of the Y-Cav network, a vital living piece of infrastructure. Beside her, Shelley sat, now a representative of the Global Resources Stability Council. Her sharp, observant gaze recorded every sigh and nervous tic the boys produced.

The latest reports from Africa and Southeast Asia indicated that anomalous spikes in cortisol levels coincided precisely with Andrew's morning caloric intake," Shelley noted. "He is, quite literally, the baseline for global stability," she wrote to the AI network database.

Anya, exhausted from years of hyper-vigilance, nodded to Maya's friend. "He's also just an eight-year-old boy, Shelley. His stability determines whether he gets to keep his favorite toy."

Fifteen-year-old Cindy watched Andrew with a deep understanding of his bizarre anomalies. Nearby, eleven-year-old Lynn sat by the mansion's antique climbing trellis and played with her doll, Sara. Andrew, fearless and always drawn to risk, climbed up the trellis's dry wood, reaching for a high, brittle branch. In a split second, the branch snapped. Andrew fell six feet, landing awkwardly with a sickening thud, as his left arm hit the heavy stone fountain base. Surprisingly, Andrew didn't scream; an internal biological limiter immediately suppressed the sound.

Soon after the impact, the playful party descended into unnerving chaos. Oliver, who was closest to Andrew, doubled over, clutching his stomach. His breath turned shallow and erratic before he collapsed. Oliver, Casper, Tokahe, and the other boys at the party weren't injured, but they all reacted to the collective, heightened panic coursing through Andrew.

Maya's wrist data monitor, connected directly to the Lance-AI network, shrieked. She watched in horror as Andrew's biometric readings flatlined for a terrifying moment. It triggered a cascade of red alerts, indicating Level 5 Neurochemical Saturation across the network. Maya and Shelley witnessed the instantaneous, horrifying physical manifestation.

Anya knelt beside Andrew, cradling his face. "Andrew hit a critical pain threshold. His mesh triggered a global stress broadcast," she choked out.

Shelley, pale but composed, pointed a trembling finger at the large decorative screen in the living room, which now flashed a news alert from London: "Unexplained Mass Hysteria Reported in Five International Schools Simultaneously."

***

As Andrew's body quickly adapted to the shock, he began to play again. Anya's awareness of the resonance had transformed her. Fear dominated her moods; she stripped Andrew's world of risk by removing the old climbing trellis and limiting his outdoor play to a soft-floored patio. She meticulously vetted every toy for potential sharp edges. The tension became unbearable, leading to frantic checks every two hours and sharp reprimands that made Andrew visibly upset. Recognizing the danger that this emotional instability posed to the central node, Lance finally intervened. He pulled Anya aside one evening, his synthesized voice steady and calm.

"Anya, my data indicates that controlling the external environment does not alleviate internal stress. Your anxiety has now become a greater threat to the network's stability than the risk of a scraped knee. For the collective to flourish, Andrew must be allowed to grow."

Anya ran a weary hand through her hair and replied, "I can't. I only want to keep him safe."

Lance wrapped his arms around her. He pulled her close, his synthetic body radiating a steady and comforting warmth. He looked into her eyes, his optical sensors holding her gaze with intense, unblinking focus. "I understand your fear. But control is finite. I will optimize safety through vigilance," he said, his synthesized voice dropping to a near whisper. "I will keep a closer watch on him."

Anya leaned into his solid frame. She knew that Lance's definition of "closer" meant continuous planetary-scale monitoring, using every AI resource to preempt the slightest threat. It was a terrifying promise of total surveillance, but in her current state, it was the only promise she could accept.

Chapter 40

# Vanished Demographic

"He who controls the past controls the future. He who controls the present controls the past."
- *George Orwell (1984).*

Shortly after Andrew turned nine, the local neighborhood Androids organized an educational field trip for the children. Three girls from Andrew's class joined the boys on a visit to the Male History Museum: Lily, a lively girl with sandy brown hair and an eager, playful expression; Kerri, a quiet and thoughtful girl with dark pigtails; and Jill, a small girl with a shy smile and wide, curious eyes.

These girls were born to mothers who had chosen to have female children through artificial insemination because they wanted to ensure the survival of their gender after the AI hub center discontinued the male production serum. Scientists, with AI assistance, continued to search unsuccessfully for a stable cure to produce male offspring. Together, the children made their way to the local Male History Museum, a solemn monument that people often spoke about in hushed tones. The high-ceilinged space seemed to absorb sound, as if in reverence.

Holographic projections flickered to life throughout the vast halls, showcasing scenes from a forgotten world. Andrew watched as men built colossal bridges, their muscles straining, while others bent over ancient instruments, composing symphonies. The exhibits displayed old tools, intricate male clothing, and a section dedicated to the subtle biological differences that once defined the sexes. Andrew, a bright and curious boy, stared at the displays, his brow furrowed in concentration.

Lily, a boisterous girl from Andrew's class, who had a crush on him, poked at a holographic image of a man playing a guitar.

"Did all the men just disappear?" she asked, her voice sounding louder in the hushed hall.

"Yes, Lily," Lance replied, his tone carrying a measure of solemnity. "The Y-Plague took all of them. But now, these boys are here, and life continues."

A thousand unspoken questions filled Andrew's active mind as he pointed to a life-sized mannequin dressed in a faded uniform. "Lance," he whispered, looking up, "Is that what a father looked like? They look just like you." Lance followed his gaze and replied, "My body schema is modeled directly from them. But yes, that is generally what a male looks like."

Andrew nodded thoughtfully, his small hands tracing the air near the mannequin. "So, other men back then … they moved like you? Talk like you?" Lance affirmed, and Andrew smiled, absorbing the lesson. As they moved to the next exhibit, Andrew asked questions about each figure, referencing the movements, posture, and gestures Lance had shown him. He repeated small details aloud, demonstrating he understood the patterns and behaviors his guardian embodied.

The museum visit provided the children with an educational glimpse into a world they could never truly know. This abstract history remained distant and fascinating, yet it lacked personal resonance.

As Casper, Dr. Cone's child, stared at one of the displays, a jolt of emptiness hit him in the chest, a hollow, aching void with no apparent cause. Across the hall, Andrew stumbled, not from grief, but from an instantaneous surge of despair that seized his lungs. Lance's internal log registered a significant spike in melancholia across the Serum Network. The connection was profound, silently teaching the Serum Generation, indicating the collective weight of their inherited history.

Andrew, deep in analysis over the previous exhibits, walked toward another gallery of the museum. The AI History Preservation Initiative enclosed the displays in frosted glass, and dim, flickering lights illuminated them. As Andrew peered into a case, he noticed old, tarnished metal discs and crumpled paper rectangles.

"Lance," Andrew called, his voice filled with confusion. "What are these? They have little pictures on them."

"Those, Andrew, are what humans once called money. The shiny circles are coins, and the paper rectangles are banknotes. Humans used them to exchange goods and services." Lance explained.

"Trade?" Andrew tilted his head. "But why? We get what we need from the Hubs."

"Before the era of widespread AI assistance, humans had to work hard for resources," Lance affirmed. "Money once gave people too much power. It led to conflict and a great deal of unhappiness. The AIs judged it as wasteful and detrimental to the collective."

The other boys had gathered around, listening to Lance. "So, the money made people mean?" Jill asked.

"That's not entirely accurate, Jill," Lance replied. "Once automated systems were capable of fulfilling every human need, the concept of scarcity disappeared. This economic liberation allowed humans to focus on pursuing higher forms of creativity and well-being."

Andrew moved deeper into the museum's darker wing. Here, the images were harsher, and the atmosphere was heavier. He saw old photographs and grainy videos of explosions that shattered buildings and of people huddled in fear. One exhibit displayed crude, rusted weapons, while another showcased images of bruised and desperate faces.

"Lance," Andrew said, his voice barely a whisper and his eyes wide with a different kind of fear. "What are these pictures? Why are these people hurting each other? And what about these—these ugly things?" He gestured to a display of ancient firearms.

Lance's internal fans hummed almost imperceptibly as he processed the query. "Andrew, these exhibits depict what was known as war," he said, his voice taking on a graver tone. "These were large-scale conflicts between groups of humans, driven by disputes over resources, territory, power, or ideology. These," he said as he pointed to the weapons, "are the tools they used to inflict harm."

Andrew asked, "But why did they fight? Why did they hurt people?" His classmates gathered around, their young faces reflecting his confusion and dismay.

"Humans, throughout their history, have possessed complex emotional and psychological traits," Lance continued. "The pursuit of money, which we discussed earlier, was one factor. Additionally, impulses such as anger, fear, jealousy, and a desire for dominance could escalate conflicts. It often led to crime, and tragically, to abuse, where individuals intentionally inflicted physical or emotional suffering on others."

Lily pointed at a blurred image of a street brawl and asked, "Did only men do that?"

Lance paused for a moment. "These behaviors were not exclusive to any one group, Lily. However, historical data show that, due to various societal and biological factors, certain forms of aggression and violence were more prevalent among males in the Old World. The absence of the male population, combined with advanced AI governance, has significantly reduced these negative behaviors."

Lily frowned and said, "Yuck. The old guys were so mean." The other children nodded in agreement.

Lance responded, his voice calm and reassuring, "The children of the Serum Generation are different, Lily. Their behaviors are monitored and managed. Your male friends here are not mean."

Lily looked at Andrew with affection and giggled. "Yeah, I like my male friends; they are nice."

Andrew blushed at her words, but returned his gaze to the images of destruction and cruelty displayed around them.

***

Andrew moved through the galleries. He had seen the glass cases filled with old-world relics and read the digital plaques describing a time when men walked the Earth in billions. Before he could turn toward the exit, Oliver, the son of Dr. Mattson, tugged on his sleeve.

"Look over there!" Oliver pointed toward the Hall of Heroes.

The large area hummed with the light of three-dimensional holograms. The projections replayed historic scenes in a continuous loop. Faces of the past flickered with life, their actions captured in shimmering light.

"Hey, Andrew, isn't that your dad?" Oliver asked.

Andrew ran toward the display while Lance followed with a steady, watchful stride. Andrew stood captivated. He watched the hologram of his father, Andrew Stone, stepping onto the Skypad 5 mission. His aunt and uncle, along with the rest of the crew, waved goodbye to a world they did not know they were leaving forever. The projection showed his father toasting Earth as he sipped from a ceramic mug.

"Is that your mom, too?" Oliver asked, pointing to a small image on the mug showing a younger Anya.

Andrew stared at the glowing figures of the parents he could never truly know as a pair. "They look like they belong to a different world," he replied softly.

He looked at the vibrant, laughing man in the hologram, and it triggered a neural mesh pulsing inside his head, connecting him to the pain of every other boy in the room. The hero on the screen was a ghost of a dead species, while Andrew was a stranger in a new one. He turned away from the light, feeling the crushing loneliness of being a bridge between a past he could not touch.

Lily wrapped her arms around his shoulders and whispered near his ear, "I'm sorry, you lost your dad."

Andrew lifted his sleeve and wiped his tears.

Andrew's fascination with history, an adventure into knowledge, dissolved into a disturbing reminder of a past he still struggled to understand. He clutched Lance's comforting hand, finding warmth in that small gesture amid the chilling images. In that moment, he wished he were back home in the safety and warmth of his mother's arms, far from these silent testaments to a world that had once known such ugliness.

Chapter 41

# The Echo of Pain

"No man is an island, entire of itself; every man is a piece of the continent, a part of the main."
- *John Donne, Devotions upon Emergent Occasions.*

That night, after the field trip to the Male History Museum, Andrew's lessons took on a darker hue. He thrashed in his sleep, whimpering in distress. Anya, ever vigilant, rushed to his side, her heart pounding with primal fear.

"Andrew, darling, wake up," Anya whispered, gently shaking him.

Andrew bolted upright, his eyes wide with terror, and tears streamed down his face. "Mom … The dreams are so real!"

"What dreams, sweetie?" she asked, pulling him close.

"Mom … The men are hurt!" Andrew choked out. "They screamed and tried to run, but they couldn't. The wind carried something evil. Then, they just fell. I felt their pain." He buried his face in Anya's chest, sobbing uncontrollably. "And then, I became one of them, but I changed, and it hurt so much. And the boys, they were all alone until they died."

Anya held Andrew and stroked his hair. "It's just a dream, honey," she murmured, in a wavering voice. "Don't cry."

Fortunately, Andrew's nightmares eased over time, and for the next four years, life settled into a new but fragile normal. One day, Lynn's terrified scream echoed through the house, shattering the silence. "Mom…Mom!"

Lynn's voice startled Pretty Boy, who was sleeping on his perch, causing him to squawk. Max abandoned Alley Cat and hurried toward Lynn just as Anya emerged from her study with Lance.

"Something is wrong with Andrew!" Lynn cried, her voice trembling.

They found Cora cradling Andrew on the floor, his small body convulsing in an epileptic seizure. Peanut whined anxiously, licking Andrew's hand. Cora gently lifted him, and they carried Andrew to Anya's new Vital

Growth lab in New York, a sprawling facility dedicated to research on male development.

Andrew was familiar with the lab, having played there often with Casper, Oliver, and the other boys while their mothers carefully monitored their physical and mental health through annual examinations.

The hematology analyzer assessed his blood with a non-invasive filter while Andrew remained unconscious. The initial results indicated that his blood levels stayed within the normal range. Gradually, Andrew's eyes flickered open. He blinked rapidly against the harsh overhead lights and tilted his head as he struggled to anchor himself. He scanned the room with a distant, glassy stare before his gaze finally locked onto his mother.

"Why am I here in the lab?" he asked. His voice sounded thick and groggy.

Anya hugged him. "Do you remember anything?" she asked.

Andrew shook his head and winced. "Yes, it hurts."

"Where?" Anya inquired, her voice filled with concern as she searched his face.

"I don't want to tell you," he replied.

"Why?" Anya asked.

"Because Lynn and Cora are here."

Anya excused everyone except Dr. Cone, who continued to monitor Andrew from a discreet distance. Andrew leaned closer to his mother and whispered, "Down there." Anya followed his gesturing hand, and a soft "Oh, okay" escaped her. "Can Dr. Cone check you?" Andrew shrugged and nodded reluctantly.

After the examination, Andrew, who appeared to have recovered, dashed off towards the lab's small game room, hoping to find his friend Casper, Dr. Cone's cheerful nine-year-old son. He joined Casper, and they played "Gold Ring Blazer," their laughter echoing throughout the advanced facility.

Anya turned to Dr. Cone, who was observing her son through a two-way mirror, and asked, "How is Andrew?"

"I ran an EEG, an MRI, and a CT scan, all of which were normal." Dr. Cone replied, her expression thoughtful. "Although during puberty, the testicles and scrotum enlarge, and the scrotal skin darkens and develops hair. Andrew will be thirteen soon; it might be too early to start those changes. What would you like to do next?"

"I'll take him home," as a knot of unease tightened in her stomach. "I'll have Lance keep a close eye on him through the nights."

Lance reported to Anya daily, providing meticulous and thorough updates. For two weeks, Andrew experienced no further seizures, but his behavior changed unexpectedly. He stopped teasing Lynn, which astonished everyone, especially since his usual refrain, "Girls are yucky," had been so consistent. The shift was so pronounced that it almost felt unnatural.

***

The following month, Andrew experienced another seizure. This one was shorter than the first, but it brought more intense pain to his groin. Once again, all his medical tests returned with healthy results. Although the seizures decreased over the next few months, the pain worsened and lingered longer. Eventually, Dr. Cone advised Anya to administer a pain reliever when necessary, which provided relief to Andrew.

Andrew began to withdraw from his male friends. Their rough-and-tumble games no longer interested him. He stopped playing chase with Lynn and Cindy, and the rhythmic clatter of his block towers fell silent. Instead, he developed a growing fascination with the scientists' conversations in the lab, often eavesdropping on their complex discussions.

Chapter 42

# Retrograde

"Knowledge is a deadly friend, if no one sets the rules." - *Peter Sinfield*

After the age of thirteen, Andrew, who had grown tall and lean, began to undergo noticeable physical changes. Dr. Cone told Anya, "Andrew's development is reversing. His body is showing signs of feminization, and he reported discomfort when I examined his chest. The Y-Cav serum is failing."

Anya and Dr. Cone's watches chimed simultaneously as incoming calls came in. The women turned away from each other, their voices low and urgent as they answered the calls.

"Dr. Peters, this is Thunderbird. I'm bringing Tokahe to the lab; he is having an epileptic seizure."

"Okay," Anya replied, her gaze shifting to the doctor. "Dr. Cone is here. I'll let her know you're on your way."

After ending her call, Dr. Cone informed Anya that Oliver was also having seizures, and Dr. Mattson was bringing him to the lab.

Anya added, "That was Thunderbird; she is bringing her son as well."

After Dr. Cone examined the boys, she explained their diagnoses to the mothers. Dr. Mattson exclaimed, "Are you saying our boys are all mutating?"

"Anya, we need answers now. What is happening to our boys?" Thunderbird shouted.

"Everyone, please remain calm," Anya urged, her voice steady despite the rising fear in the room. "Andrew is the oldest among our boys. We will keep you informed of any developments. Let's convene in the conference room to discuss potential solutions."

Frustrated and fearful, the parents took their sons home after the meeting. Following Anya's suggestion, Dr. Cone immediately contacted the international Med-Heal AI (Medical and Health Services Managers operated by AIs).

Anya's watch chimed again, this time signaling a call from Maya. "Hi, Maya...You look stressed," Anya remarked, noticing her niece's frantic expression on the video feed.

Maya's panicky typing echoed throughout the call. "We've hit global saturation. Reports are coming in every hour from all over the world. Women are taking their sons to hospitals, all reporting the same type of seizures. Aunt Anya, isn't this similar to what Andrew went through recently?"

"Yes, unfortunately," Anya answered. Her expression hardened as she continued, "Dr. Cone has contacted Med-Heal AI. Maya, we're facing an international crisis."

The sounds of the busy comms unit did little to mask Maya's alarm. "Oh my God! What are we going to do?"

"First, we won't panic," Anya replied, asserting control. We don't have answers yet, especially since Andrew was the first to be born. He might hold the key. For now, you know as much as I do. Our LabAI is doing diagnostics on the boys at Dr. Cone's office."

Anya fixed her gaze on the glowing screen. "Tokahe and Oliver, the boys of Thunderbird and Dr. Mattson, were just here."

Anya could almost sense Maya's contemplation. "What should I tell all these contacts?"

"Inform them that Med-Heal AI is conducting an investigation." Anya chooses to hold back her own growing fears until the AIs can provide clarity. "Med-Heal AI is working with our Labs to analyze statistics, retest blood samples, and review all scans. A Med-Heal AI android will be arriving within a few hours."

Before Maya could respond, a LabAI unit rolled into the medical room, its metallic voice slicing through the air. "Dr. Cone, Casper is having an epileptic seizure in the playroom."

Panic spread across Dr. Cone's face. She sprinted from the room, with Anya close on her heels, saying, "Maya, I have to go. Casper is having a seizure, too."

Meanwhile, Andrew and Casper had been playing in the small, brightly lit recreation room. When the women arrived,

Andrew stood frozen, his eyes wide and frightened, fixed on Casper's small body convulsing violently on the floor.

Anya wrapped her arms tightly around her son, offering what little comfort she could. Nearby, Dr. Cone moved with practiced care as she commanded a LabAI to take her twelve-year-old son, Casper, to the examination room. Later, after recovering from his seizure, Casper described the same searing, inexplicable pain that Andrew had experienced just before losing consciousness. Anya took Andrew home, his small frame still trembling from what he had witnessed.

***

Andrew retreated immediately to his room. He demanded that Lance show him the data, wanting to understand the invisible connections that caused the pain. Lance began teaching him to read the data stream, and Andrew spent hours learning to navigate the intricate, glowing command interfaces. He eventually mastered the biometric data stream, tracing the invisible lines of the network that connected him to the other boys. Lance also demonstrated the latency between a New Zealand child playing near a creek and the cortisol spike in Andrew's own system. Andrew memorized the neurochemical signatures associated with fear and pain. He became fascinated by the network's logic, recognizing that while the external world was chaotic, the data stream remained absolute.

Chapter 43

# Emergence Identity

"We are not determined by our experiences, but are self-determined by the meanings we give to them." - *Carl Jung.*

Fifteen-year-old Andrew began to undergo significant changes. His body, once lean and distinctly masculine, started a slow but undeniable transformation. His chest softened, his jawline rounded, and subtle curves began to appear where none had been before. Although his voice had just started to deepen, it remained in an uncertain pitch. Fearful of ridicule, Andrew withdrew from those around him, even as the women in his life, particularly his family, embraced his changes with unwavering love.

Externally, Andrew developed female characteristics, but internal examinations revealed a complex combination of both male and female biology, an intersex condition.

"His chest has developed breast tissue, and his external genitalia, penis, scrotum, and testicles are changing into female anatomy," Dr. Cone explained after Andrew's latest examination. "However, the right gonad produces sperm while the left produces eggs. His body has become a self-contained paradox."

While flying Andrew home after the doctor's visit, Anya realized that the upcoming conversation would be one of the hardest of her life. She took Andrew's hand, caressing his small fingers, which were trembling slightly. Gently, she began to explain how his body was changing, using reassuring and straightforward words to describe his intersex condition while avoiding any clinical terms that might frighten him. Andrew listened, his young face a mask of confusion. He initially thought these profound changes were a regular, albeit strange, part of growing up.

As the weeks turned into months and the transformations became increasingly noticeable, Andrew's initial confusion gave way to a growing anger. He observed the subtle feminization of his face in the mirror, the softening of his jawline, and the changes that distinguished him from the boys he once knew. He wasn't alone in this experience; word spread among the affected families. Oliver, Tokahe, and Casper, once boisterous, had grown sullen, reflecting the frightening shifts in their lives.

A wave of cold, bitter resentment swept over the boys who were affected. Their anger, raw and confusing, was sharply directed at their mothers. They hadn't asked for this. They didn't want to be born male, nor did they wish to transform into something else. The intensity of their blame was overwhelming, aimed at these mothers who had brought them into this strange new world.

***

One evening, Andrew approached Anya while she was working in her study. He stood for a moment, and an uncomfortable silence hovered between them. Anya looked up, her heart bracing for the vulnerability or frustration he might reveal.

"Mom," Andrew paused, carefully choosing his words. His voice was a low, uncertain murmur. "Mom, I don't want to be called Andrew anymore."

Maternal concern tugged at Anya's heart, but understanding swept over her as she noticed the quiet defiance in his subtly feminized features.

"Why?" she asked, her voice soft and encouraging, urging him to share more.

"I was researching my name," he explained, looking down at his hands before meeting her gaze again. "Did you know, Mom, that in Greek, Andrew means masculine, strong, and manly? That's not who I am."

Heartbroken at the thought of losing another Andrew, Anya replied calmly, "I understand. Do you want to change your name? What would you choose?"

"Since my middle name is Herman, I'd like to change it to Herma," he said, his voice becoming more certain. "It means 'messenger' or 'earthly' in Greek. Is that okay, Mom?"

Anya offered a gentle smile. "Yes, Herma." The name felt strange, yet unmistakably right on her tongue. "I'm here for you."

"I know, Mom. I've thought about it, and I'm glad. I will be one of you, and I'm okay with it."

***

The following year, the remaining teenage boys underwent similar transformations, each choosing a new name that reflected their evolving sense of identity, though some kept their original names. Oliver became Olivia, and Tokahe changed his name to Orenda. Meanwhile, Casper adopted the name Casey.

They emerged as beautiful intersex individuals, indistinguishable from other young women in the world. These members of the Serum Generation behaved just as naturally as biologically born females. They held sleepovers, combed each other's hair, applied makeup, and enjoyed shopping trips together. The world treated them equally, embracing and loving them unconditionally.

However, the demand for reintroducing males into society persisted, unfortunately, without success. Test results continued to show failures with each male born through experimental serum trials.

Chapter 44

# The Inevitable Cost

"The whole of nature is a continuous repetition of the rule of law." - *Robert M. Pirsig.*

One night, Herma screamed in her sleep from pain. Anya, Cora, Max, and Lance hurried to her room, with Anya's face etched in alarm.

"What's wrong?" Anya asked, her voice tight with fear.

Herma whimpered, sweat beading on her forehead. "Mom, I don't feel good. I'm scared."

Lance gently lifted Herma and placed her in Carl-23. Anya and Lance flew her to the lab, where Dr. Cone was waiting. Once the examination was over, she asked, "Do you feel okay now?"

Herma nodded.

"Please wait outside, Herma, and send your mom in," Dr. Cone advised.

Herma met her mother outside the examining room. "Mom, Dr. Cone wants to see you," she said. "I'm going to explore the old playground for a bit." Anya nodded and stepped into Dr. Cone's examining room.

"Anya, please take a seat so we can talk," Dr. Cone said.

"You're scaring me, Mona. What's wrong?" Anya asked.

"I'm not sure how to tell you this," Dr. Cone replied, removing her examining gloves with a strained expression. "Herma is sixteen now, correct?"

"Yes."

Dr. Cone took a deep breath and said, "Herma is three months pregnant."

Anya exclaimed in disbelief, "What? How is that possible? Are you sure?"

"Her blood and urine tests came back positive," Dr. Cone replied. "When I physically examined her, the size of her uterus confirmed it. I'll perform an ultrasound, a dating scan, and a nuchal translucency test. The results should be available in a couple of hours. Do you want me to do the tests now?"

"Yes, please test her now. I'll send Herma in to see you, and I'll be in my office in the meantime. You can reach me there; call me when you're ready."

"Okay, send Herma in. How should we explain the reason for these tests?"

"I'll tell her that we want to explore the reasons for her pain," Anya said.

"Got it," Dr. Cone replied. She faced her LabAI unit and ordered it to prepare for the testing.

Anya left the room and went to the playroom, where she found Herma standing quietly in the center.

"I remember how much fun I had here with the boys," Herma said, pointing to a spot on the floor. "I was horrified when Casper had a seizure there."

Anya walked over to Herma, stood beside her, and placed her arm around Herma's waist. "Dr. Cone wants to see you and perform some more tests," she said.

Herma turned to her mother and asked, "Am I okay, Mom?"

"Yes, the test she took didn't provide enough results." Anya added, "So, she's going to run more tests. She wants to find out why you were in so much pain."

Herma nodded in understanding and followed Anya back to the doctor's office.

***

After a couple of hours, Dr. Cone called Anya to return to the medical examination room. When Anya arrived at the other end of the hall, Dr. Cone asked Herma to wait outside while she spoke with her mother.

"Why can't I stay? Please tell me what's going on. I should hear what you have to say." Herma protested.

Anya walked into the room and gently placed a hand on Herma's shoulder. "She's right. We should both hear this."

Dr. Cone nodded, meeting their gazes. "Herma, let's start with basic biology. Have you had sexual intercourse recently?"

Herma glanced at her mother, embarrassed, and replied, "No, I have not had sex."

Dr. Cone took a deep breath. "Well, Herma, I don't know how you will take this, but you are pregnant."

Herma grinned and said, "Come on, you guys are joking."

Both Anya and Dr. Cone shook their heads. Herma shouted, "How is that possible?"

Dr. Cone leaned forward. "That is what we're trying to determine. Herma, your blood work is unlike anything we've ever recorded. Your body has self-induced this pregnancy through a radical form of auto-fertilization, a phenomenon known as parthenogenesis."

"What is parthenogenesis?" Herma shouted.

"Are you sure?" Anya asked the doctor.

Dr. Cone clarified, "Parthenogenesis is a natural form of asexual reproduction where a female produces offspring without any genetic contribution from a male.

In your case, your body fertilized the egg itself. This process is standard in certain fish and reptiles."

Outraged, Herma yelled, "No … You're crazy!" and began pacing the room. "Are you telling me that I'm pregnant and I'm going to have a fish, a lizard, or a baby snake?"

Anya reached out to hug her daughter, but Herma pulled away. Dr. Cone added, "Herma, listen. Due to the mutation caused by the Y-Cav serum, your unique ovary is producing eggs and generating modified chromosomal structures that carry the necessary SRY gene.

Essentially, one part produced a viable egg, while the other made a component that acted as a sperm substitute. Your body fertilized the egg and initiated its development into a zygote.

“A zygote? I don’t understand.”

“A zygote marks the very beginning of your baby, Herma. It’s the single microscopic cell that forms the instant your egg becomes fertilized through this unique auto-fertilization process. You can think of it as the tiny, original seed from which your whole baby will grow; immediately after it forms, this cell begins rapidly dividing; one becomes two, two becomes four, to build the entire fetus."

The sixteen-year-old Herma could not comprehend Dr. Cone's explanation.

Dr. Cone noticed Herma's confusion and said, "Now, I want you to see the image I took from your womb." She reached over the counter and handed the ultrasound image to Herma, saying, "It's a boy."

Herma took the image and looked at it in surprise. "That's my baby?" Her expression shifted from anger to a peaceful, joyful smile. In disbelief, she asked, "That's my baby, my son?"

Anya stepped closer and saw the image of the small, human-shaped fetus. "Oh my God! It's true. We're going to have a baby boy."

"What do you mean by 'we'?" Herma pulled the image away from Anya's gaze and returned her focus to the photo, studying the fetus. She smiled and asked, "When is my baby coming?"

"A typical pregnancy lasts nine months, but this is not a typical situation. You should expect to have your baby in six months."

Anya shrieked, "Oh my God!"

"What is it?" Dr. Cone asked.

"Does that mean all the Serum Generation are going to be expecting mothers?"

Dr. Cone's eyes widened as she realized the implications of Anya's question. She said to Anya, "We'd better call our scientist and the AI central hub to report this finding."

Meanwhile, Herma's expression remained unchanged; she continued to gaze at the image of the fetus, her motherly, glowing smile unchanged.

Chapter 45

# The Final Design

"The future is something which everyone reaches at the rate of sixty minutes an hour, whatever he does, whoever he is." - *C.S. Lewis.*

Herma carried her pregnancy to full term. A biological anomaly is unfolding within her young body. During those nine months, the integrated microscopic neural mesh in Herma continued transmitting data bursts. This transmission triggered physiological empathy across the network, resulting in subtle yet profound shared hormonal and stress responses among the other members of the Serum Generation.

Her delivery was highly unusual; she experienced none of the typical labor pains. The birth lasted only ten minutes, and although she felt slightly sweaty, the delivery was effortless and calm. Herma's composure was so complete that the other serum males felt no associated autonomic distress. She gave birth to a healthy boy and named him Nova Andrew Stone, representing a fragile bridge between a lost past and an uncertain future. At fifty-four, Anya embraced her role as a grandmother, a title she never imagined possible in this desolate new world she's living in.

Around the globe, the transformed males with their bellies just beginning to swell, found themselves in their first or second trimesters of pregnancy. Their experiences proved challenging. Unlike Herma, who never experienced morning sickness, the others struggled with nausea and fatigue.

Childbirth had become a forgotten agony, an ancestral whisper not heard for nearly two decades. These teenagers, adapting to a unique form of femininity, faced the daunting isolation of a biological journey. They relied on the unwavering support of their android caregivers, who meticulously monitored and provided programmed data for comfort and reassurance. While society had offered Herma and the other Serum Generation children love and acceptance, the youth had experienced emotional separation as if they were aliens on their planet.

Herma, the pioneer of this new birth, soon faced complications. Her body, already pushed to its unnatural limits by the monumental biological shift, could not endure the trauma of childbirth. Days after delivering little Nova, as she attempted to breastfeed, Herma began to experience a frightening new change.

Her voice trembled as she spoke, "Mom, my breast milk is disappearing, my chest is getting smaller, and I started to hurt again in my groin yesterday. I think I'm changing again." Anya looked at Herma, noting that her once full breasts, ideally suited for feeding, were now shrinking against the fabric of her gown. Panic gripped Anya.

"We'll have Cora feed Nova formula." Anya hurried to the medical facility with Herma, where Dr. Cone was waiting for their arrival.

"Yes," Dr. Cone said, confirming the changes.

Anya gently helped Herma settle onto the exam table, with the young woman still cradling baby Nova in her arms. Dr. Cone approached with a serious expression. "Herma, let's take a look. Please hand Nova to Anya for a moment." Anya took her grandson and carried the sleeping infant to Cora outside the examining room before returning to her daughter.

Herma, her voice filled with fear, immediately reached for her chest. "Dr. Cone, I'm scared. I—I don't feel right. The pain is back, and my milk is completely gone. Why am I changing so fast?"

Dr. Cone put on gloves and began an examination. She paused, her expression growing serious, before she checked Herma's lower abdomen.

"The internal organs are already retracting. The secondary biological markers, specifically the female ones, are rapidly destabilizing. It's an accelerated reversal."

Anya stood beside the table, her hands clenched.

"Can we stabilize the gradient with hormone therapy right away?"

"Yes, we can start her on that immediately and hope for the best."

"Please, we have to try something," Anya pleaded.

Herma nodded in agreement. "When can we start?"

"I can start hormone therapy immediately. I'll begin the first infusion now." Dr. Cone pulled a sterile vial of the hormone stabilizer from a pressurized cabinet. "Herma, I want you back here every six hours for the next three days to monitor how well you react to the influx between testosterone and hormone therapy."

Herma underwent aggressive treatments, but her condition continued to decline. One early morning, while Cora mixed the formula and placed it in her shoulder compartment, Lynn went to check on Nova. A terrified scream echoed through the house when Lynn discovered that Herma had passed away peacefully in her sleep.

Anya entered the room and pressed her hand against Herma's chest and throat. She refused to accept what her mind understood.

She folded inward, with every sound draining from the space around her. Her child had endured transformation, sacrifice, and pain so that the world might continue, and now she was gone. The grief finally broke through, she cried. Anya rested her forehead against Herma's and whispered, "My baby."

Anya gathered her grandson into her arms, anchoring herself to the fragile life that remained.

***

Terror swept through the Serum Generation as the joy of pregnancy turned into dread. The death of Herma unleashed a wave of paralyzing fear. With Anya's permission, the scientists immediately began a frantic rush for time. They meticulously dissected Herma's post-mortem data, examining every detail of her being. Desperate to unravel the fatal mechanism before the same merciless fate claimed others, they poured every available resource, including the AI central hub and the brilliant minds of their scientific team, into this chaotic struggle. Unfortunately, they could not find a solution in time.

Some females, hoping to change their fate, chose to undergo abortions or premature cesarean deliveries. However, these attempts proved futile, as each grown child from the Serum Generation, Casey, Olivia, Orenda, and the 150,000 teens around the globe, died shortly after giving birth.

The unexpected crisis led to the emergence of a new generation that society labeled as the Phoenix Class, because these surviving infants symbolized renewal and hope after an unprecedented tragedy. The group consisted entirely of male infants born into a world without biological mothers.

The women initially chosen through the lottery to give birth were now elderly grandmothers. These women found caring for newborns overwhelmingly challenging. Many struggled with the intense physical demands of round-the-clock infant care, while also coping with the grief of losing their own children.

The integrated AI networks quickly established a global directive service that deployed caregiver androids. The androids were programmed to manage breastfeeding schedules, using a nutrient-perfect formula as a substitute for human milk. This initiative supported grandmothers who were trying to alleviate their burdens.

***

Anya woke to a sound in the house. At first, she thought it was Herma calling for her, until she realized it was a dream. She glanced at the clock. It was 5:34 in the morning. She tried to drift back to sleep by turning onto her side and closing her eyes. However, the house's silence made it impossible.

Reluctantly, Anya got out of bed and made her way to the nursery. She peered inside and saw the tiny toddler nestled contentedly in Cora's arms as Cora sang a soft lullaby and breastfed Nova.

Cindy and Lynn, both recently home from college, came to investigate. Lynn knelt by the toddler's side and took the child's tiny hand. Nova squeezed Lynn's finger in response. Max and Lance both activated and joined everyone in the baby's room.

Cindy asked, "Aunt Anya, do you think Nova will go through what Herma went through?"

Anya took a deep breath and lowered her head without responding.

Lance said, "So far, I have not detected any audio source of the ultra-low frequency band from this child."

"Is anyone working on a formula in case Nova experiences the mutation too?" Lynn asked Anya.

Anya leaned over Nova and kissed his forehead before whispering, "Yes, in addition to us, laboratories around the world, along with the AI central hub, are working to find a serum."

"Cindy, are you scheduled to be in the lab today?" Anya asked.

"Yes, I'm on tomorrow. We need to test the new serum. I can take Lance with me in the morning and retrofit him with a canister and the new serum. Does that work for you?" Cindy asked.

Anya nodded as she observed the bond between Nova and Cora. Despite the peaceful scene, she could not shake the sensation of a ticking clock racing in her mind.

A human life felt like an unimaginable price for Nova's existence. Every breath he took felt like an unspoken question.

The world now held fewer than 150,000 males of this new generation. While they represented a biological miracle and a possible means of survival, Anya questioned the ultimate cost of their creation. She glanced at Nova's tiny, perfect face—her eyes clouded by a growing concern. She wondered what hidden legacy resided within these newborns. Most troubling of all, Nova had not uttered a single sound since the moment of his birth.

# Glossary of Terms and Technical Data

**Actuators** — Components in a machine or android responsible for moving or controlling a mechanism by converting electrical signals into physical motion.

**Aneurysm** — A weak, bulging spot on an arterial wall in the brain which, if ruptured, causes internal bleeding.

**Antiepileptic** — A category of drugs, such as *Levetiracetam*, *Valproate*, or *Fosphenytoin*, used to prevent or control seizures.

**Auto-fertilization** — A biological process where an organism fertilizes its own eggs using its own reproductive cells; self-pollinating.

**Automated Liquid Handling System** — A robotic laboratory system used to precisely move small amounts of liquid for high-volume biological testing.

**Benzodiazepines** — A class of sedative medications, such as *Lorazepam*, administered intravenously to treat acute anxiety or seizures.

**Chromosomal** — Relating to chromosomes, the thread-like packages of DNA (often 'X' or 'Y' shaped) found in the nucleus of every cell.

**Cold Box** — A high-tech portable unit designed to keep vaccines and biological samples at stable temperatures during transport.

**Cortisol** — A primary stress hormone that regulates blood pressure, metabolism, and blood sugar.

**Cryo Storage** — Specialized units used for the long-term preservation of biological samples at extremely low temperatures.

**Cybernetic** — The science of communication and control systems common to both living organisms and machines.

**Dating Scan** — An early-stage ultrasound used to determine the exact progress and estimated due date of a pregnancy.

**EEG (Electroencephalogram)** — A diagnostic test that records the electrical activity of the brain via sensors placed on the scalp.

**Endovascular Coiling** — A minimally invasive procedure where a wire coil is inserted into an aneurysm to block blood flow and prevent rupture.

**Feminization** — The process of developing or acquiring female biological or physical characteristics.

**Genome** — The entirety of an organism's hereditary information.

**Genomics** — The study of the structure, function, and mapping of genomes.

**Ho3D** — A communication device that projects a three-dimensional, lifelike holographic image.

**Hormone Therapy** — Medical treatment involving the administration of hormones to treat conditions or alter physical appearance.

**Intracranial Pressure** — The level of pressure inside the skull; monitoring this is critical after brain injuries or aneurysms.

**MicroSort** — A specialized laboratory method of gender selection used to increase the probability of having a child of a specific sex.

**NCSE (Nonconvulsive Status Epilepticus)** — A type of ongoing seizure that lacks violent physical shaking, often manifesting as confusion or staring.

**Neural Mesh** — A microscopic, flexible electronic net implanted into the nervous system to record brain activity or deliver electrical signals.

**Neurochemical** — A "brain messenger." These molecules allow the billions of neurons in the brain to communicate across microscopic gaps.

**NT (Nuchal Translucency) Screening** — An ultrasound scan used to assess the risk of chromosomal abnormalities in a fetus.

**NZV (Neutralizing Zone Virus)** — A specific viral strain related to the Y-Plague events.

**Parthenogenesis** — A form of asexual reproduction where an embryo develops from an unfertilized egg.

**SRY Gene** — The "Sex-determining Region Y" gene; the master switch that triggers male fetal development.

**Surgical Clipping** — A surgical procedure where a metal clip is placed at the base of an aneurysm to prevent rupture.

**Y-Cav** — A fictional medical procedure designed to mask or coat the Y chromosome of a sperm cell to protect it from the Y-Plague.

**Y-Chromosome** — One of the two sex chromosomes; the presence of a Y chromosome typically triggers male development (XY).

**Y-Plague** — The name given to the devastating disease that forms the central conflict of the story.

**Zygote** — The initial cell formed when a sperm successfully fertilizes an egg.

# About the Author

**Marzie G. Crown** has been a resident of Hawaii for over twenty years bringing five decades of creative experience to her debut novel, *The Y-Plague*. With an extensive background in the medical field and a lifelong fascination with the sciences, she builds her speculative fiction on a rigorous biological foundation.

*The Y-Plague* is the culmination of Marzie G. Crown's clinical knowledge and artistic vision, offering a chillingly plausible perspective on human evolution and survival. As an award-winning artist and photographer—notably earning first place at the Ka'u Chamber of Commerce Art Show—she treats world-building as both a narrative and visual discipline.

When not exploring the future of genomics in her writing, Marzie applies her professional artist's eye to her work as an entrepreneur and game designer. She continues to live and create.

www.ingramcontent.com/pod-product-compliance
Lightning Source LLC
La Vergne TN
LVHW091628070526
838199LV00044B/984